I0638380

SOUTHERN JUSTICE

Ricardo S. Dubois

Edited by: Angela Hooper

Back photo courtesy Dwight Moore

SOUTHERN JUSTICE

ISBN: 978-0-6151-7232-3

SOUTHERN JUSTICE

Chapter One

Early morning in the Georgia swamp has the beauty and serenity of few places on Earth. Moss-clad cypress trees conceal the source of the beautiful sounds emitting from them. Many species of songbirds all joined in joyful competition. Frogs joined in, completing the symphony with their deep croaks blending in with the constant cricket noise in the background.

The light early morning fog seemed to break the encroaching sunlight into several individual beams of light, each emitting from a single source.

This day, however, was not a day in which one could contemplate the meaning of life in this serene setting. This was to be a day of training for the Secret Tactical Intervention Group of the United States, also known as STING.

For all practical purposes, these men did not exist, their entire identities long since erased. Their training was much more intense than that of the Navy Seals or Special Forces. The key prerequisite for admission to the group was not to have any next of kin, of any kind. No one to miss you after you disappeared, no one to ask or pursue an explanation of your disappearance.

Today was to be a day of training in the swamp. Nothing out the ordinary for a group whose entire career had been spent in the most adverse conditions imaginable, but were still able to come out of it unscathed.

The commanding officer, though proud of his team's success, had been concerned with their increasingly overconfident attitude. It was now time for the team to be humbled. To show them that no matter how good you think you are, there's always someone better.

With a thunderous, "Attennnntion", the serenity of the swamp was broken as the young STING Captain brought his group of three to order.

The STING forces had come well-prepared with the latest in electronic weapons used to simulate a kill on their opponent. Dressed in tiger stripe camouflage, black berets, and black leather boots that laced up to the knee, these men were ready to conquer the challenge that lay before them, like they had done so many times before.

The Captain yelled out an "At Ease" command, then began to address his men.

"Men, today you will be attempting to locate, isolate, and immobilize one man in the swamp," the Captain paused, looking over their green and black camouflaged faces.

The STING group looked at each other as though amused at the thought of only having to immobilize one man. For a team trained to immobilize many men at the same time under a great variety of conditions, this seemed like it was going to be a walk in the park.

The Captain continued, "You will each be given an armband, in the event you are immobilized, you will relinquish your armband. The purpose of this exercise is to return with your opponent's armband, realizing a minimum of casualties," the Lieutenant concluded. "Are you clear!"

"Sir! Yes Sir!" The group yelled, without hesitation.

"Then bring me back an armband!" the Lieutenant yelled.

The men turned and started into the dark swamp, each going in a different direction.

The gentle glow of a fire built on one of the few areas of high ground in the swamp provided warmth to the man that would soon be hunted by one of the country's most elite forces the United States had to offer.

Lieutenant Shad Boudreaux was a large man at six feet three inches, and tipped the scales at an even two hundred pounds. He had chiseled good looks and the charm and charisma to match. His good looks were not what separated Shad from so many others. It was his knowledge of the swamp and his trapping and stalking skills that was what made him such a sought out individual. Shad would prove to be an adversary like none other his opponents had ever faced.

Lieutenant Shad, when not helping to train STING members, commanded a Seal team specializing in reconnaissance missions. Whenever the United States Government suspected a country of either terrorist activity, or a military buildup, and it was unable to confirm its suspicions through satellites, it became necessary to send someone in to confirm it; Shad's team was usually sent in. He was quite proud of the fact that after several missions, all of which being very difficult, he had never lost a single man in his command, and had always been able to complete his assignment. Today, Shad's task was to immobilize and capture the STING team, retrieving their armbands in the process.

Dawn approached in the swamp gradually, like the sands of an hourglass, each grain of sand emitting a little more light until at last, darkness was no more.

Shad began to prepare himself for the day's activities; strapping on the laser sensor suspender that he secured tightly. Checking the knife he had sharpened to a razor's edge, this would be the only weapon he would bring on this exercise. He had done this many times before; each time hoping his opponent would present a more challenging adversary. Yet each time being disappointed by the ease at which he brought them down.

The swamp had now began to lighten in advance of

the early morning's sun. He prepared himself, both mentally and physically, then began to search for one of the ambush sites he had selected the previous day.

Locating a cypress tree wider than his shoulders, and with a variety of different size cypress knees, Shad settled down with his back against the tree, submerged with only his head exposed from the nose up. Patiently he waited, as he peered through the cypress knees looking for movement, and listening for the telltale sounds, which to the trained ear is like setting off an alarm. Soon his prey would be near, and like the alligator who remains motionless until his prey is within striking distance, Shad would not be detected until it was too late.

This particular location chosen by Shad had special significance. Located just off a natural trail, a path through the water unobstructed by cypress knees, it would more than likely prove to be too tempting a path for at least one of the STING team, also because this particular cypress tree was special. Peering through the cypress tree knees, a distant movement could be detected. It was one of the STING team coming straight down the path heading straight toward him.

SOUTHERN JUSTICE

Chapter Two

When the STING team entered the cool swamp water, it was not quite light yet. Aiding in the perpetuation of the early hour darkness was the tall cypress trees with their full canopy overhead.

Splitting up in order to cover more ground and also to terminate this exercise as soon as possible, each STING member took his bearings then headed out. Armed with their high–tech, scope-mounted laser rifles, a quick kill seemed imminent. After all, all they had to do was spot him and shoot him, it wasn't like they had to capture him.

John was the youngest of the team at nineteen. John took a northern bearing, then: cautiously moved out into the swamp water, gradually becoming more and more in tune with his surroundings as the sounds of the other STING members slowly faded away. He tried to concentrate on the mission, but could not help to momentarily reflect back to the events that had brought him to this swamp.

At ten, John lost his parents in an auto accident, and for the next eight years, he was shuffled from foster home to foster home. At eighteen, John joined the army and was soon recruited into special operations.

When STING was created, John fit the profile of the

perfect candidate. With no family ties, John could cease to exist and no one would miss him. That was the thought that troubled him the most, above killing or dying was the fact that he no longer existed. No record of any kind could be found on him. Only in the darkest, deepest corners of the Pentagon would any mention of his existence be found. This gave the Pentagon plausible deniability in the event of a failed operation. Even if one of them were captured, nothing could be traced to the Pentagon, no matter what they said.

Cautiously moving through the swamp, John recalled his jungle training; through practice, he was now able to evaluate the sights, sounds, and feel of the objects around him without being distracted by any one sense. A split-second distraction had proved fatal for many a solider who allowed himself to be distracted.

Walking through the swamp was not at all what John had expected. He had mentally pictured wading though chest deep water, while being bogged down by the soft bottom. Discovering waist deep water with a hard bottom was a welcomed revelation.

Cypress trees and various other small trees varied in thickness according to the location. Some cypress trees were close together with the knees protruding well away from the base, making passage very difficult if not impossible.

SOUTHERN JUSTICE

After walking through the swamp a while, John began to discover some natural paths not cluttered with cypress knees, which made forward progress easier. Moving along at a steady pace, John continued down the unobstructed path nature had provided for him.

The congested placement of trees made long-range visibility virtually impossible. John proceeded slowly, scanning the distance for any movement or anything that would seem to be out of place. As he approached the largest of the cypress trees, he made a quick scan of the area then paused, as he looked up in awe at the size of the tree.

The closer John got to Shad's hiding place, the more Shad was able to distinguish his features. Shad thought he was extremely young; between eighteen and twenty, he seemed out of place to Shad, not having worked with anyone that young in quite a while.

In the distance, he moved cautiously, observing each and every leaf and tree that surrounded him. Still closer, Shad continued to observe him, making a mental calculation of how much ground was covered by his prey in a given time. Closer now, Shad squinted his eyes so as to block the white in his eyes. Shad calculated he was traveling roughly twenty yards every minute. Twenty yards away, now Shad took a deep breath then slowly submerged beneath the surface of the murky water and began to feel and listen to the vibrations caused by his prey as he moved. If everything went according to plan, at one minute and five seconds, his prey would be right upon him.

A minute and five seconds seems a lot longer when you're holding your breath, but it quickly passed as Shad felt the vibration of his prey making his way through the water getting stronger and stronger then stopping right by Shad as he reached the minute mark.

Shad began a slow assent till his eyes broke the surface of the water. Shad's luck was far better than he had hoped for, standing not more than three yards away was the STING team member, he had stopped, and was looking up in the trees.

John heard the splash of water, as something large tore to the surface from its submerged hiding place. Before John could wheel about, he was grabbed from behind and pulled backward into the swamp.

John struggled but his opponent was too strong for him to break his grip, then just as quickly as whatever it was that had grabbed him, he was released to the surface.

Struggling to regain his footing, John soon stood in a defensive position, scanning the area for a target. To John's surprise and disgust, there was no target.

Perhaps he was still under the water, John thought as he prepared for the sudden appearance of the unknown phantom, but none came. John began to scan the area once more in a 360-degree sweep, looking and listening but nothing could be seen. John looked around all the nearby cypress trees, thinking the attacker sought cover behind one of the trees, but nothing was found. It was as though the attacker had appeared out of nowhere and disappeared the same way. John looked down at his arm, half knowing what he would find. His armband was gone!

John felt humiliated, he had been taken out of the exercise in less than five seconds and never knew what hit him. John did not know who, or where this ghost solider was, but one thing was sure, he had just developed a great deal of respect for him. He and the rest of the team were considered the best of the best, and to be immobilized in five seconds without even a shot or a fight was unthinkable.

John looked forward to seeing who could appear and disappear without a trace, but for now, he was out of the game, and so he started the long walk back to base.

Remaining motionless in his underwater hiding place, Shad listened and felt the vibration of his adversary walking out of the swamp, getting farther and farther away.

After Shad had dragged John under the surface of

the swamp and removed his armband. Shad had swum underwater to a large cypress tree that had a hollowed out center, forming an air pocket.

The swamp, like rivers and bayous, are subject to low water periods. When the water had fallen below the root structure, air was allowed to enter the hollow cavity and was then trapped there when the water rose. This was what Shad had looked for; a large enough cypress with an air pocket next to a natural trail, and it had paid off.

When the sound of the STING member could be heard no more, Shad left his hiding place and headed for his next ambush sight.

SOUTHERN JUSTICE

Chapter Three

Lieutenant Fred Parker was the second member of STING that would fall prey to one of Shad's traps.

Parker, a tall slim man of thirty years, looked like someone who should be running up a basketball court, rather than running through the swamp. Reaching a height of six feet, eight inches, he stood like a giant in comparison to John.

Parker had been recruited into STING for the same reasons the others had; that being not having any family ties. When Parker joined, he first joined the Navy right out of high school and had pressured the Navy for more challenging assignments. Parker, having an outstanding service record and no family to speak of, was another perfect prospect for the STING team.

From the beginning, Parker had excelled in every part of the STING training, from academics to the physical demands that were put on his body. He possessed an uncanny ability to second-guess his adversary, he would pose a formidable challenge to Shad.

From a distance, Shad paralleled Parker's movements. Parker was heading right for one of his traps when he lost sight of him in the thick cypress trees. Shad however, was still able to track his movements and direction. Even after all the STING training, the group had not learned to walk quietly through the swamp. This was how Shad was able to follow his movements.

Unlike Parker, Shad would raise his foot just high enough to clear the hard bottom of the swamp floor and slowly bring his leg forward in a slow steady motion. No splashing, very little noise.

Parker scanned the landscape for any potential threat. It's an uneasy feeling knowing you're going to be attacked, but not knowing when or where.

Parker's movements were slow and deliberate, although noisy. His eyes did not miss a clue or sign that would reveal any potential danger. A broken leaf, or a scraped stump, all signs were evaluated.

Parker stepped forward, like he had done so many times before shifting his weight to his forwardmost foot.

Too late! As Parker shifted his weight, he realized his mistake, but it was too late. The 3/8" cord tore through the surface of the murky water as it was pulled to its upward destination.

Parker had triggered a snare that was operated by a cypress tree which gave every appearance of having been previously struck by lightning. It was approximately 24" in diameter and had been broken off about 20 feet in the air. With its severed trunk leaning against its natural mate, and the top of the tree resting in the water. It had appeared the tree was simply an unfortunate casualty of nature. This, however, was not the case. Someone had transformed this scene into a trap.

Running the rope and trigger mechanism along the bottom of the swamp and up the side of the tree, the severed tree would provide the energy to catapult its snared victim from the floor of the swamp into the air above the water.

As Parker was jerked upward, the severed cypress finally completed its descent to the swamp floor, echoing its loud splash through the swamp.

Sometime during the initial assent, Parker's rifle was jerked free from his grasp and disappeared below the water's surface.

Suspended with his head above the water, Parker rotated as he hung from his precarious position. Then in the distance, he saw movement. A man, completely camouflaged, was heading directly toward him. His movements were steady and deliberate with no sound. If Parker had not seen him, he would not have known of his presence.

Shad had watched as his snare pulled Parker upward. He also saw Parker lose his rifle in the water. With his prey immobilized and without a means of defense, Shad moved in to claim his armband.

Upon Shad's approach, Parker began bombarding Shad with questions.

"Very ingenious," Parker said as Shad approached. Parker did not take defeat well, having know it so few times in his life. But this time he did manage to swallow his pride enough to accord Shad the respect he deserved.

"How were you able to find the time to set this trap up?" Parker asked still unable to initiate a response from Shad.

Tearing off Parker's armband, Shad slowly pulled his bowie knife from his boot.

Parker knew this was only a training exercise, but being in such a defenseless position was something Parker had never experienced before. Always in the past, he had been able to defend himself in some way or another, until now. Parker continued to twirl totally helpless.

With his razor sharp knife, Shad cut the rope that held Parker prisoner. With a loud splash, Parker was once again earthbound, struggling to get to his feet.

"Find your rifle and get back to camp," Shad said, as he turned and headed south to meet his third and final quarry.

Parker got on his knees, reaching with both probing hands, trying to retrieve his submerged rifle. While searching, Parker reflected on how quickly the recent series of events had transpired. It was a humbling experience for him.

Trudging his way through the swamp, stopping and listening more than he walked, Shad was trying to determine a direction in which his next victim could be located. Shad walked and listened for an hour, till finally in the distance he could hear the faint sloshing of a man walking through the knee-deep water.

Shad quietly moved in closer and positioned himself. With his back against a cypress tree, he waited. He could hear the STING member rather well now and he knew exactly how far away he was. What he had to determine now was a direction of travel. Shad would have to move ahead of him and take him out by hand. It didn't take long for a direction to be determined. The STING member was moving at a noisy but steady pace. It was apparent just by listening to the excessive noise produced that the member was getting tired. Headed in an easterly direction, Shad was off to maneuver in front of him.

Hart was the last member of the STING team remaining in the swamp. A former college football linebacker, Hart weighed in at 250 lbs and was pushing a height of 6'-4". Broad-shouldered and very muscular, Hart was stereotypic of the American fighting soldier.

Hart followed a natural path that had been the case

throughout the swamp. Lanes less cluttered by roots, which made travel for a tired solder much easier.

In position now, Shad waited. Hart progressed toward him; twenty yards ahead, a large fallen cypress tree lay across the lane, with about two thirds of it in the water. On each side of the obstruction lay thick cypress with many protruding roots. Hart, weary from the morning's activity, saw this fallen tree as an ideal resting spot and headed toward it.

Upon reaching the fallen log, Hart lay his rifle across the tree, in a perpendicular fashion, then climbed on the log, laying back with his fingers interlocked behind his head to form a pillow.

Hart was not too concerned about being attacked, he felt sure he could hear anyone approach. Upon any approach, he could be in a defensive posture in seconds. Gun at his head, Hart closed his eyes and listened to the sounds of the swamp.

In position, and what a position it was. He had anticipated Hart stopping to rest, and since this log presented the only dry area in sight, he had positioned himself under the log, with his head exposed up to his nostrils for air, Shad was concealed on the backside of the log as Hart approach. This would be perfect, Shad thought. He would be able to secure his third armband without much resistance.

Remaining motionless as the distant sound of sloshing water moved ever closer, finally, the source of the sound had arrived. Shad pressed against the log and clung to the swampy bottom, only exposing his nostril and eyes. Shad saw the rifle being placed on the log, its long barrel protruded past the log finding a point of balance as it lay ready. The electronic sensor mounted on the rifle tip had not been called upon to decide an adversary's fate yet, but that would soon change. Shad's ear pressed so close to the log, every sound and movement generated onto the tree conveyed forth to his ear. He heard Hart as he hopped onto the tree and lay across its back. He saw the protruding elbow past the width of the tree, with his armband within inches of him. This left no doubt to the position Hart was in.

Slowly and quietly, Shad moved toward the rifle. His forehead pushing through the water making tiny ripples as he advanced. Reaching a point directly under the rifle, Shad's arm broke the surface of the water and moved in a straight vertical path, so as not to allow any water droplets to noisily return to their source of origin. By keeping his arm straight, the water would quietly slide back down his arm, returning quietly back to the swamp.

Reaching for a point on the rifle that would be as close to the center of the rifle as possible, Shad lifted,

Hart's rifle, and keeping it in a horizontal position, he guided the rifle away from the log. Keeping the rifle steady, Shad stood up and stepped back from the log.

Hearing the intentional noise Shad had made, Hart sprung up and reached for his rifle, which was no longer there.

"Looking for this!" Shad said, as Hart turned to face him.

The bewildered look on Hart's face said what his words did not. Totally shocked at how Shad could have snuck up on him so quietly, staring down the barrel of his own rifle, Hart just shook his head in total disbelief.

Shad removed Hart's armband and tucked it away in his pocket with the others. Removing the electronic power pack that powered the laser, thus rendering the rifle useless. Shad tossed the rifle back at Hart. "Return to camp!" Shad instructed, "The exercise is over.

"What about the others?" Hart questioned, unwilling to believe the entire operation could have ended so soon.

"You were the last," Shad said, responding to his question. "I'll meet ya'll back at camp, I need to do some cleaning up out here first," Shad said, referring to a couple of more traps that had been set, but not sprung. Shad headed through the swamp, back to the campsite he had used the night before, he still had his backpack and machete there.

By the time Shad had reached the campsite, he had already removed his electronic vest and was carrying it in his hand. Placing the vest in the canvas backpack, he scanned the area for his machete. Retrieving it, he placed it in the sleeve mounted on the side of the pack.

Pulling the pack onto his back, he started walking once again in the swamp, heading back to the meeting point where the STING team waited.

Returning to the base of the STING team, Shad found his former adversaries comparing notes among themselves. As Shad approached their commanding officer, he spoke to Shad.

"I was told my men wouldn't put up much of a challenge for you, but I didn't believe it." The Captain paused for a moment as though waiting for Shad to interject something.

Shad remained silent to this point, he too was waiting, waiting for the Captain to finish so he could get back to Fort Benning and begin his leave.

The long-winded Captain continued to ask questions, delaying his departure even farther.

"You were able to immobilize all three in less than three hours, that's amazing," said the Captain, reiterating the obvious.

After saluting the Captain, Shad reached for his outstretched hand to shake it.

"Your men are good," Shad said, looking over his shoulder to the three STING team members standing a short distance away.

"But they need to spend more time in the swamp, practicing concealment, detection, and for their own safety, learn how to walk through the swamp quietly." Shad suggested a couple of manuals that were available through Special Forces, which he had contributed to the writing of.

"These manuals I feel could help your men," Shad said. The Captain thanked Shad, shook his hand once more and then he walked to his men.

Choosing not to approach the team, he started to walk away; Shad always kept all training on as impersonal a basis as possible.

Looking over his shoulder, he simply nodded at the team and started toward the clearing where he had left his transportation.

Chapter Four

Going to the baggage compartment of the Bell Lone Ranger helicopter, Shad removed a towel and a change of clothes, replacing them with the soiled wet ones.

Shad, besides being extremely proficient in land activities, was also able to fly just about everything in the air, from helicopters to jets.

The engine roared into obedient compliance, as the rotor blades began to slowly rotate in a counterclockwise motion, gradually generating more and more speed finally reaching its idling speed.

Lifting off, he quickly rose above the swamp. Shad was always amazed at the contrast the swamp had from the air. It appeared like any other forest would appear from the air, tightly placed treetops concealing its forest floor. But from the ground, it was a completely different story. Leveling off at 3,000 ft. and a speed of 110 knots, Shad manipulated the joystick till he had the desired heading.

Ft. Benning was only about 30 min. away by air, Shad thought, as he pointed the aircraft toward the base. As he passed over tiny communities, he thought about the people below him. Communities whose entire population was probably born, raised, and probably would die there. People whose entire travel experience had been to the nearest large town. Shad reflected on how these small communities so closely paralleled his own home.

Shad was born and raised in the Atchafalaya, an area in south Louisiana where the swamps are measured in miles, not acres. Shad was the only child of Cajun parents, whose roots could be traced back to the early 1800s. This was when his great, great grandfather was exiled from Nova Scotia, for not embracing the king's religion. Devout Catholics, he and his family chose to be exiled rather than change religion. His great, great grandfather left Nova Scotia with the clothes on his back, like many others who left. Traveling southward, they came to settle in an area of south Louisiana which would later be known as Acadiana. This was a rich area, where fur-bearing creatures abound, and fish were in huge supply. Shad's great, great grandfather was a barrel maker by trade, and he opened a shop which provided he and his wife a good living. During the depression, Shad's dad was forced into the swamp to survive. The swamp provided everything they needed; food, shelter, and clothing.

Born in the same cypress cabin his grandfather had built, Shad was taught the ways of the swamp from his grandfather and dad, and he felt more at home in the swamp than he did anywhere else. When he was ten, his dad moved to St. Martinville after the death of his mom. This allowed Shad to expand his limited horizons. From the one room schoolhouse, he had to travel a mile to reach, to a modern school with excellent facilities to broaden young minds.

Shad's life took a new direction when he was introduced to a friend's brother who was on leave from the Marine Corps. Talking for hours about all the places he had been, the places he had seen, it was around that time the desire to see more of the world than just south Louisiana began to grow within him. After consulting his father, Shad was reluctantly given his blessing to join the Navy after high school. Upon completing basic training, Shad was given the opportunity to try out for the Seal teams. Only one out of one hundred made the teams. This elite status appealed to Shad.

Having no difficulty completing the course, Shad was soon assigned to a team where he and four other men performed covert operations throughout the world.

Shad had never been idle and constantly sought challenges when the routine became too mundane. He learned to fly, and pursued this passion as much as his limited time would allow. From helicopters to jets, Shad became proficient at each and every one of them.

Shad's elite status as a swamp expert came much later. During a training exercise, his Seal team was placed in the swamp, surrounded by a platoon of marines, and was instructed to split up and evade capture. Each member of the team was captured, but one.

Maneuvering through waist-deep water proved too difficult for most, and concealment even harder. With so many men looking for you, there was only so many places you could hide.

For two days, the platoon searched for him and was unable to find a single clue. Without food or water, the officers felt sure he would return to camp and surrender before they had to call him in, thus saving them face. This was not to be the case. The exercise was terminated and with the use of a bullhorn, Shad was ordered in.

Forty-five minutes passed before Shad returned to camp. Expecting to see a tired, hungry, worn-out soldier dragging his feet in camp, the awaiting soldiers got a sharp contrast.

Shad strolled into camp with a rested look on his face and a bounce in his step. Reporting to the commanding officer, Shad stepped to attention as he saluted. Shad gave his name, rank, and team code number.

The officer eyed Shad up one side and down the other, obviously still frustrated from his denied victory.

Noticing blood on Shad's sleeve, the Captain asked if he was injured and what was the source of the blood.

Shad's response caught the commander totally by surprise.

"Lunch!" Shad briefly responded.

"Lunch!" yelled the Captain, "And just what did you have for lunch?" the Captain asked in a sarcastic tone.

"Frog, sir, they were delicious," said Shad, trying to keep his responses as brief as possible.

Not wanting to go into Shad's eating habits for the last couple of days, the Captain switched gears.

"How were you able to avoid the whole platoon for so many days?" asked the Captain, at this point more puzzled by this man than agitated.

"I hid, sir," Shad's answer was short and simple, as had been the case from the beginning.

"We searched every inch of the swamp, there was nowhere for you to hide," the Captain responded, still just as puzzled.

"I know you did, sir," said Shad. "Many of your men walked so close to me, I could have reached out and touched them. On two occasions, they almost stepped on me," Shad concluded.

"Where did you learn to hide like that?" the Captain asked, a lot less sarcastically and more respectful of Shad's ability.

"My father, sir. He and I used to work and play in the swamp, he taught me everything I know," Shad replied.

"This has never been accomplished before," said the Captain. "We're usually able to round everybody up pretty quickly, but you were never found." The Captain paused for a moment before asking his next question. "How long could you have stayed out there?" the Captain asked.

"Till you called me in," Shad responded.

"That's not what I asked you," the Captain said. "How long!" the Captain said, repeating his original question.

"Meaning no disrespect, sir, till you called me in." Shad repeated his original reply.

"You mean to tell me you could have stayed out there for an indefinite period of time with no food or water?" the Captain questioned, unable to fully grasp the full extent of Shad's ability.

"There's plenty of both out there, sir, but to answer your question, yes, sir." Shad could see the Captain was having a hard time believing him but there was little else he could offer to convince him.

"Shad, I'm going to ask your Commanding Officer about allowing you to work with our book department writers, to formulate a training manual in which you might be able to share some of your skills so more could benefit from your knowledge, would you be willing to do that?" the Captain inquired.

"Yes sir," Shad responded.

SOUTHERN JUSTICE

From that point forward, Shad was known as the best swamp rat in the service and was loaned out as a consultant and trainer on swamp training exercises.

On the horizon, Shad spotted Fort Benning. The base had an unmistakable appearance from the air, an awesome sight to a tired soldier. Being on loan from the Navy, Shad stuck out like a sore thumb, and had sensed the hostility from some of the men. It wasn't because they had anything against Shad. They just didn't like Navy boys in their Fort.

Making contact with the control tower, Shad was given landing instructions, and he descended the aircraft to 1500 ft. to begin his approach.

Shad would be coming in on runway 4. As with civilian Airports, army bases required helicopters to take off and land down runways. This was to avoid any chance of midair collisions. Landing the craft and allowing a cool down time for the helicopter to return to idle temperature, he knew from flight school that cooling down too quickly would cause excessive wear in the engine. With the rotor blades completely stopped, Shad exited the craft and secured the blades to the tail. Retrieving his bag from the luggage compartment, he headed for the parking lot. It had turned out to be a beautiful day and Shad once again got excited about his leave.

In the overcrowded parking lot, Shad's car stood apart from the rest. Not only was it the only one like it in the parking lot, it was also the only one of three ever made. He had found the car, a 1970 Judge convertible with a 455 high output engine by accident, while stationed at Fort Polk, Louisiana. While on leave, Shad had been traveling home, but instead of traveling the same route he had taken many times before, he had decided to go a different way to experience a little different scenery. While passing an old farmhouse, Shad had noticed a car partially covered with a tarp. The hood and half the windshield was exposed and Shad could see the car had been in a wreck. Even though the front end had been smashed, it was still recognizable as a Judge.

Stopping, Shad had approached the owner. As it turned out, the elderly man's son had been killed in the accident and to be rid of the yellow beast just suited him fine. Shad had picked the car up for a mere five hundred dollars, and towed it back to Fort Polk in a rented car hauler. Restoration had taken a whole year, working on it every free moment he had.

When complete, the car had truly become the car of his dreams. Its bright yellow exterior was contrasted by its rich-looking black interior. It was a beauty.

Unlocking the car door, Shad tossed his bag in the back seat, and climbed behind the wheel. Turning the key, its powerful engine roared to life. The presence of power seemed to just ooze from the car.

Shad's car was without a doubt the fastest, most powerful automobile on the base. Shad never made a habit of bragging about his car, but whenever challenged Shad was quick to put all would-be kings in their place. A flash, and the smell of burning tires was all any challenger ever saw of Shad after he left the line.

He headed toward the barracks where he would shower, shave and changed his clothes into civilian.

This was the first day of his thirty-day leave. He was to travel back to Louisiana, where he would help his dad with the tour business. While there, he also hoped to take in some fishing. It had been quite a while since he and his dad had wet a hook together.

After showering and dressing, Shad packed the few remaining articles that had not been previously packed in advance, and closed the large green canvas suitcase. Carrying his suitcase to the car, Shad placed it in the trunk then headed to see his Commanding Officer. A quick report on how his assignment had gone, then Shad would be on his way.

Skipping several steps on the way to the raised building, he stepped into the outer office of Captain John T. Brooke. Entering, he was greeted by a young pretty redhead named Anna.

"Well, good morning to you too," came the snappy greeting, as Ann just looked at Shad, as though hurt that he didn't speak to her sooner.

"Good morning, Anna, how's my favorite secretary doing today?" said Shad, trying to make up for his preoccupation with other matters.

"Oh, now I'm your favorite secretary, am I?" Anna said, still on the offensive. "When was the last time you called your favorite secretary?" Anna continued, still trying to keep Shad off-balanced.

Anna and Shad had dated for a while and had turned into great friends. Anna would often call Shad to talk about anything and everything. It wasn't long into the relationship that they both felt a strong bond with each other, but it was more of a brother and sister kind of relationship. After they both came to terms with this, their friendship grew even stronger. Hardly a week went by without Shad calling Anna. Lately, however, Shad had been very busy and had been unable to contact her. This was what she made reference to this morning, playing to Shad's guilt.

"I'm sorry, Anna, things have been crazy lately, can you find it in your heart to forgive me?" Shad asked, waiting for an affirmative answer.

Instead, Anna chose to keep him hanging a little longer.

"The captain is on the phone, would you please have a seat," Anna said, avoiding Shad's question and indicating to him that she was still unhappy with him.

Not being in too playful a mood, Shad decided just to let her cool down a bit, he would approach her again later.

Shad should have been tired from being up all night but he wasn't. The excitement of going home had generated an enormous amount of energy. His pacing the floor in front of Anna's desk began to make her feel uneasy. Realizing this, Shad decided to examine the photographs on the office wall.

This was not the first time he had seen these photographs. On many other occasions while waiting to see the captain, the pictures had been examined. A signed photo of the President held a place of honor, surrounded by smaller group shots of different men and different battles that the captain had participated in. Many of the captain's battles would never be known, most of which were covert and top secret. Such was the nature of their business.

Anna motioned to Shad that the captain was off the phone and that he could go in. Shad winked at Anna as he entered the office, which brought a half-smile to her face. Entering the room, Shad saluted the captain.

"Have a seat," the captain instructed, gesturing to a

chair in front of his desk.

"How did your exercise go with the STING unit go?" asked the captain, as he walked around his desk and sat down.

"About like usually," Shad said, trying to be evasive.

"Yea right," the captain said, "I'm glad you went, those STING guys are a cocky bunch. I'd have liked to have seen them brought down a notch or two. Anyway, what else is on your mind, Lieutenant?"

"Nothing sir, I thought I would check in with you before leaving," said Shad.

"Leaving?" the captain replied in a surprised tone, then remembering the authorization approval for Shad's leave.

"Going any place special?" the captain asked, not necessarily being nosy, just curious.

"Home, sir," Shad replied without hesitation.

"How is your dad, Shad?" asked the captain.

"Well, sir."

"Is he still operating that tour business?"

"Yes, sir."

"My wife has been after me to vacation in south Louisiana, I think this summer we might go down and look your dad up," said the captain as he pulled out a pipe and tobacco pouch and began filling it.

"He would be pleased, sir, but you might get more

than you bargain for, he has a reputation of a talker," Shad reminded the captain with a broad smile.

After a few more minutes of chitchat, the captain wished Shad a safe journey. Shaking the captain's hand, he left the office and headed for his car, anxious to get on the road.

It was two o'clock before Shad left Fort Benning. He calculated he would probably be able to make it about half way home before having to stop for the night. His dad did not know he was coming down a couple of days early, and was going to surprise him.

With the radio blasting a country and western song and the top down, Shad pushed the Judge to a cruising speed of 75 miles per hour. The sky was clear and blue. The warm summer breeze blew the top of his hair as the scenic landscape passed quickly by. Shad looked forward to seeing his dad again, it had been a while.

SOUTHERN JUSTICE

SOUTHERN JUSTICE

Chapter Five

The sun was just starting to peek through the moss-clad cypress trees, as Jean Boudreaux secured his airboat to the dock. Tying both the bow and stern, Jean took special care not to allow too much play in the line. The tranquil bayou gave a false sense of security, as it offered no visible threat to the aluminum craft. However, on more than one occasion, speedboats had used the straight stretch of bayou in front of Jean's house and business as a racetrack. The fast speedboats were a constant disturbance to the peace and calm the bayou offered. They also were a menace to any boat that had the misfortune to cross their path. The wake generated by these boats had damaged Jean's boats in the past, and now he tried to take every precaution to prevent it from happening again. On one other occasion, one of his boats was sunk when the stern slid under the dock while it was lowered in the valley of the wave. Since then, Jean had been meticulous about securing his boats.

His airboat, which he used the most, was secured parallel to the dock protected from damage by old tires attached to pilings. His other boat was a converted covered party barge that was lined with rows of old church pews, which he had obtained when the local church replaced them with new ones. The U-shaped dock that surrounded the party barge on three sides was also secured with rubber bumpers. The dock was on the same level as the barge floor to facilitate easy boarding. From the water, the dock took an upward incline to the office and parking lot.

The parking lot was extra large, big enough to park two or three tour buses. His office, a bland white structure, made no attempt to project itself as a professional business establishment. In fact, the only way it was not mistaken for a small cabin was the 4'x8' sign Jean had mounted on the roof.

The sign read:

JEAN BOUDREAUX SWAMP TOUR

Full of color, the sign had birds, alligators and other wildlife pictured in a swamp scene, with Jean as the centerpiece, push polling a pirogue.

As Jean walked through the door of his office, a small bell mounted on the door announced his presence. Mrs. Galliano, Jean's secretary, assistant, and all around tour coordinator, looked up over her bifocals as Jean walk in.

"How was your trip," she asked, leaning back in her oak swivel chair.

"Ok," Jean answered, " I found a new area full of wildlife to take the tourists. Did you hear from Shad?" he asked, with an anxious tone.

"Not a word, when are you expecting him?" Mrs.

Galliano asked.

"Don't know the exact day, he said sometime this week," Jean replied.

"Oh, by the way, we have a tour bus coming tomorrow for a tour," Mrs. Galliano informed her boss. "Eight o'clock, early for tourists, huh?"

Mrs. Galliano was extremely punctual, and in all the months she had worked for Jean, she had never been late for work. What she had always had trouble with, however, was understanding why anyone on their vacation would want to get up so early.

Mrs. Galliano was like many of the people in the small town. A vacation was something you used to relax and sleep in, not to go gallivanting all over the country. The largest town Mrs. Galliano had ever seen was Lafayette, and that had only been on a rare occasion. All her life, her entire world consisted of a ten-mile radius, and she saw no need to change now.

"But that's the best time in the swamp, it's cool and the swamp has not quite woken up yet," Jean explained, trying to express upon her what would motivate tourists to awaken so early. Mrs. Galliano listened, but was not swayed.

The one-room office building was only a little larger than a large bedroom. In it were two oak desks, one was Mrs. Galliano's, and the less cluttered of the two was

Jean's.

Mrs. Galliano handled all matters of the business such as advertising, scheduling, etc. Since Jean hired her after her retirement as a teacher, and the recent death of her husband, she had been a godsend. Jean only had a fifth grade education and lacked much of the knowledge required to successfully operate a business on a daily basis.

However, what Jean lacked in book sense, he more than made up for in the ways of nature. No one knew the swamp better than Jean.

Sitting at his desk, Jean picked up the phone to call an old trapping buddy of his. The phone rang several times before finally being answered.

"Hello!" the grisly old voice shouted.

Speaking in Cajun French, Jean began to converse with his old friend.

"Tee Nag, I caught you in the middle of something?" Jean asked.

Claude Breaux, long-time friend of Jean, had lived in these parts as long as Jean had. A trapper by trade, Claude had earned a reputation as an outlaw. Spotlighting deer was his specialty. Using high power lights to blind the deer, then as the animal was mesmerized by the light, Claude would take aim at the animal.

No one really knew how he got the nickname "Tee Nag", it was just one of those things that stuck to him, and that was what Jean had called him all his life.

"Ah, it's you, Jean, I was working outside on my net, how you been doing, haven't seen you in a while, How's Shad?", asked the old trapper, not realizing he had asked so many questions without waiting for an answer.

"He's well, he's coming down this week on leave," Jean informed his friend.

"Carry him by here to see me when he comes."

"I will, Tee Nag," said Jean, pausing a while to make sure there was nothing else Tee Nag had to say.

"Tee Nag, the reason I'm calling, I want to ask you about them helicopters traveling in the swamp."

"Yea, I know which ones you're talking about. I've seen them going back and forth. Don't know for sure where they're going, but rumor has it somebody is setting up operation at the old Slickco plant." The last few words from Tee Nag were a bit muffled as he took the opportunity to spit out the juice from his chew.

"You mean the one they shut down?" asked Jean, puzzled over the fact that anyone would want to reopen the plant. All known producing wells had long since dried up.

"Yea," Tee Nag continued, "I was out that way last week. Keep out signs were at least every 50 yards all the way around. All bayous leading to the refinery have been dammed up with the exception of the main entrance, which has a guard tower."

"I wonder what's up?" Jean asked. "We always got along good with the local oil companies, a lot of times we would go eat lunch with the guys stationed out there."

"You're right, Jean, but I don't think these new guys are oilfield," Tee Nag said as a tone of concern entered his voice. "I saw a couple of them in town the other day at the Fast Stop, they had a Spanish accent," Tee Nag said, not having to explain why they stuck out. Most everyone around St. Martinville spoke French, to introduce another language or accent into this area was as good as hanging a sign from your neck, you stuck out.

"When they went to check out," Tee Nag continued, "One of them pulled out a wad of hundred dollar bills. It seemed quite out of place for this area," Tee Nag said, as he could be heard relieving himself by spitting his tobacco juice.

"And something else I've been noticing," said Tee Nag, "A lot of strange people have been coming in and out of the area."

"Well this is the tourist season, Tee Nag," said Jean, trying to keep Tee Nag's imagination and suspicions in check.

"These people were not tourists!" Tee Nag interjected

in his own defense. "They were always men, and were in groups of two or three, most tourists we get are family or retired."

Jean understood Tee Nag's reasoning, but was not ready to jump to any conclusions, not yet.

"How about the sheriff? Have you had any contact with him?"

"I don't talk to the sheriff, you know that," said Tee Nag, making reference to his many run-ins with the local law enforcement over poaching. "If it were up to him, he would run me out of the parish. Ever since he caught me on the old Slickco site hunting them turkeys."

"What happened?" Jean asked, thinking it unusual not having heard about it before. Not too much went on with the people of the small community that Mrs. Galliano didn't know about, and in turn couldn't wait to tell Jean.

"He told me that the new owners did not want anyone trespassing, and if I knew what was good for me, he had better not see me around there again. He meant it! Since then, him and his bully deputies have been watching me like a hawk," concluded Tee Nag, making no effort to conceal the agitation in his voice.

"Something seems funny around here, Tee Nag. Too many new faces without a specific purpose. Maybe I might take a run by the old plant, and see what our new neighbors are up to," said Jean.

"You be careful, Jean, I've seen them men with guns and they didn't seem shy about using them," Tee Nag cautioned, knowing his warning would not be heeded. He'd known Jean for too many years. Once something got under his skin, Jean stuck with it until it was resolved. One way or another.

"I will, Tee Nag," Jean said, in a halfhearted attempt to reassure his friend, knowing it would do no good. "You take care now," and with that Jean hung up the phone.

Jean's attention was drawn to the noise emitting from outside his office. Very faint at first, then gradually increasing in intensity. A sound he was very familiar with; it was the unmistakable sound of one of the SPEEDBOATS!

Chapter Six

Jean opened the curtain just in time to see the red speedboat zip by, its blown engine threw a characteristic rooster tail of water a little higher than usual, as it raced its way home.

"Damn race boats!" Jean said, as he turned to Mrs. Galliano, who had not gotten out of her chair. The speedboats had become so familiar to Mrs. Galliano that she hardly even noticed them any more.

Jean turned to Mrs. Galliano.

"Has your boy heard anything about the old Slickco plant reopening?" Jean asked, walking away from the window and towards Mrs. Galliano.

Mrs. Galliano's son worked as an oilfield consultant for many of the large oil companies in the area. He had become invaluable to companies wanting to drill and purchase land from the locals. Not only did the local residents distrust the oilfield lawyers, all dressed up in their three-piece suits, they wouldn't even talk to them.

That's when Jeff Galliano was called in. By talking to the locals in their area, Jeff was able to negotiate some rather lucrative deals for several local landowners. It was also quickly understood by the oil companies where his loyalty lay. Jeff would make every attempt to stay impartial, but when he felt the company was trying to rip-off his people, that's where he drew the line. He would first go to the company and try to negotiate a fair price on his own. If that failed, he would refuse to make the offer to the landowners. Jeff lost a great deal of money doing this over the years, but one thing he never lost was sleep, feeling guilty for what he had done. Little went on in the oil industry without Jeff knowing about it, after all, that was his business.

"You know, funny you should ask," said Mrs. Galliano. "I did call him just the other day because I wanted to know about all the helicopter activity in the area. He said the old Slickco Plant that had been up for sale, well, none of the major oil companies wanted it, saying all the reserves had been depleted. Jeff thought this was strange because of the miles of pipeline that could be easily tied in to offshore facilities, thus prolonging its life. There was only one serious offer by an independent oil company, but they were unable to get financing. Slickco Oil had all but resigned itself to the fact that they would not be able to sell it, and would eventually just have to abandon it to the State. Last month, an oil company out of Columbia made Slickco an offer far better than they had expected, and took over the property." Mrs. Galliano paused for a moment then continued to freely offer the information Jean had requested.

"No one really knows what their plans are, they have released all the employees that were on standby, and have not advertised for replacements," said Mrs. Galliano, finally concluding all the information she had available for immediate recall.

"Strange?" Jean said, thinking out loud, "Very strange."

Jean went back to his desk and pulled out a map of the surrounding area. Most of the Atchafalaya he knew like the back of his hand, but the Atchafalaya was a huge area and there was no way for him to know every inch.

Stretching the map across the desk, he scanned the map looking for the point of interest. There it was, the old Slickco oil plant.

The plant was relatively close as the crow flies, but to reach it by boat was quite a different story. Jean noticed there were only three canals running into the facility. All three were manmade to tee off into two main bayous in the area. The three canals offered one way in and one way out.

Folding the map several times until only the plant and the immediate area was displayed, Jean scanned over it. Reaching into his desk drawer, Jean used paper clips to secure the map in its folded position. This was a must when traveling. Nothing was more aggravating than fighting with a map as the wind whipped it to conform to its instructions.

"Mrs. Galliano, I think I'm going to take a ride out to that plant and see what it looks like." Jean said, as Mrs. Galliano peered over her bifocals. "I should be back by late afternoon."

"You be careful, Jean, I don't have a good feeling about that place," said Mrs. Galliano, trying to persuade Jean to use caution.

"Is that your women's intuition kicking in again?" Jean asked with a broad smile. Mrs. Galliano was always coming up with intuitions about everything under the sun, Jean would usually smile and agree with her. Only then would he be allowed to continue unharassed.

"Call it what you want, something is just not right about that place," said Mrs. Galliano, waiting for Jean to reassure her.

"Mrs. Galliano, I promise I'll be careful and if I start getting that bad feeling, I'll come straight home, I promise,"

Jean agreed, holding up his right hand as though he was preparing to be sworn in.

With Mrs. Galliano reassured, Jean left the air-conditioned office into the warm and humid early morning. Jean quickly put on his shades, as the sun caught him by surprise.

SOUTHERN JUSTICE

While closing the office door, a horn blast from an old nineteen forty-two Ford pickup truck summoned his attention. Paul Domangue's old pickup truck was just coming over the one-car wooden bridge. The noisy steel plates that were laid across the treated timbers provided both a smooth path for the tires, and a means to prevent wear to the timbers.

Paul turned into the oversized parking lot and began bringing the vehicle to a stop. The noisy brakes screeched their need for repair, as the truck finally came to a complete stop.

In the truck, Paul was accompanied by his wife, Cotile. A large woman with a heart twice her size, Cotile had been Jean's wife's best friend and had stayed with Jean by her side till the last day when cancer finally claimed her. Cotile and Paul were very poor, but proud people who would give you their last piece of bread if you needed it more than them. As proud as they were generous, they had never taken handouts from anyone.

Paul had built a shack on the edge of the Atchafalaya not far from where Jean had been raised as a boy. A trapper and fisherman by trade, Paul had had a couple of bad years. The price of pelts was far lower than before, and he had gone past his credit limit at the general store. Things seemed like they couldn't get any worst. Then tragedy hit when Paul's only son of 10 years old was lost while swimming with friends at their regular swimming hole.

An encroaching alligator had latched on to the young lad, drowning him. Up till that time, no alligators had ever been seen in the area and it had been considered safe. Devastated by the loss, and unable to pay for a proper funeral they were at a loss.

Jean, upon hearing of the incident, went to Mr. Thibidaux's mortuary and paid for the entire funeral arrangements. Jean cautioned Mr. Thibidaux that no one was to know who had paid for it, Mr. Thibidaux agreed and fulfilled his obligation.

Paul did not have to narrow the field down too far to figure out it was Jean who had made the arrangements. His signature was all over it. So many times before when the people in the community was in trouble, he had come to their aid requesting that he remain anonymous. However, in such a small community, loose lips soon spread the word.

Jean had done well with his tour business and being alone, he did not require much money to live on. It made him feel good to be in a position to help his friends.

His friends never forgot him, always bringing him homemade pies, and during crawfish season, he always had more than he could use.

Jean walked up to the passenger side of the truck,

greeting Cotile first, then Paul.

Speaking to Paul in French, Jean asked, "How do you do, Paul?"

"I do well, old friend," said Paul, nodding his head as he spoke as though to reassure himself that he was telling the truth. "How are you?" Paul asked, kicking the question back to Jean.

Jean simply responded, "OK."

"I hear you need cypress to build a gazebo for your tourists?" Paul questioned, visibly catching Jean off guard.

"Yes," said Jean, stumbling over his words at first then quickly regaining his footing. "It would give them a place to rest, eat, and wait, while they shopped the local stores," he said, regaining his composure once again. The question had caught Jean off guard because he himself had only come up with the idea two days ago.

"I got cypress, I will bring you next week, two truck loads," Paul said, as he straightened himself back up in his seat.

"Great!" Jean said, "I'd rather buy them from you than the lumber shop."

"I will not accept pay, Jean, you know that," said Paul, showing Jean this was his way of helping him for a change.

"I know," said Jean, "I thought I'd offer."

"OK," said Paul as he put his truck into first, "I'll see you next week."

Jean waved goodbye then started down his dock to the airboat.

Climbing in, Jean placed the map on the seat as he turned the ignition switch, reawakening the sleeping beast once more.

Casting off both bow and stern lines, Jean climbed into the high mounted driver's seat, keeping the map under one leg for quick reference.

Double-checking the bayou for traffic then stepping on the floor pedal, he inched the craft forward. The engine whined as the large wooden blade sliced through the air, steadily increasing in speed.

Chapter Seven

Jean made good time on the bayou, the warm summer air blew his gray hair straight back as the boat slid effortlessly through the water.

After about an hour of traveling at top speed, Jean came to the first of the three canals that led to the plant. Jean knew the first entrance had been blocked, but what he wasn't prepared for was the manner in which it had been blocked. The first entrance had been used as a scrap iron dump. A sunken iron crew boat was poised as the centerpiece of the twisted maze of old flowlines and assorted scrap. This entrance had been very effectively barricaded. It would take two men equipped with cutting torches a full day to cut a path wide enough for a boat to pass.

Jean looked at the map and sought a path for the next canal. Ten minutes later, Jean was at the main entrance.

The entrance looked more like an army outpost than a plant entrance. The high guard tower lookout was manned by two camouflage-clad individuals maintaining a vigilant lookout both day and night, judging by the large floodlights mounted on the railing.

As Jean slowly crept by the entrance, a large steel gate came into view. Electronically operated, and spanning the entire length of the twenty-five foot canal, it rose above the water's surface to a height of five feet. Mounted on each side of the fence were bright yellow signs with red letters which read:

WARNING

RESTRICTED AREA

NO TRESPASSING

The two tower guards stared hard at Jean as he inched his way past the entrance, never taking their eyes off of him until he was completely out of sight.

Consulting the map one final time, Jean navigated to the third and final entrance. Reaching the last entrance, Jean's expectations had been confirmed. The last entrance had been filled in with shells, closing off the entire entrance. The shell barrier spanned the entire entrance, rising to a height of three feet above the water line then tapering off at the front and back.

Jean eased the nose of the airboat into the shell embankment, the shells noisily scraped the airboat's metal bottom. Shutting off the engine, Jean picked up his binoculars. Walking toward the front of the boat, he also picked up the paddle and bowline to secure the boat. Jean pulled the bowline taut. Using the paddle as an anchor, Jean tied the bowline to the center of the shaft, then positioned it on the opposite side of the levee, covering it with shells.

Taking a position at the top of the levee, Jean scanned the area trying to orient himself to a direction. In the far distance, the plant could be seen, from this distance it looked relatively unchanged.

Then Jean spotted it! There it was; the speedboat which had ripped past his house for the past several weeks. Jean put the binoculars to his eyes, first focusing on the speedboat. The high speed craft was empty, its bow tied to the shore.

The canal had been dredged out of the swamp by cutting down the cypress trees then dredging out the canal and stacking the unearthed dirt on one side of the canal, forming a man-made levee from the entrance of the canal all the way to the plant.

Jean focused in on the plant, the thick band of cypress trees which lined the canal allowed only a narrow window for him to observe any suspicious activity.

The noonday sun beat down hard on Jean as he patiently stared through the binoculars. Jean studied the plant intently, stopping only to wipe the sweat from his eyes.

The swamp was unusually quiet, hardly a sound could be heard. Not even a gentle breeze was felt to offer a brief reprieve from the afternoon temperatures. The swamp assumed an uneasy calmness.

Very faint at first, fading in and out, Jean thought he heard a noise, a very faint noise. Setting the binoculars on the ground beside him, Jean stood up and listened, trying to determine a distance and direction. Making a complete 360 degree turn, Jean knew it was coming from the direction of the plant.

Starting down the levee that paralleled the canal, Jean took care to be constantly vigilant of his surroundings.

The sound was growing stronger, clearer now, Jean recognized it as a man screaming in pain, screaming for help, pleading for mercy.

Jean started running now to the source of the sound. Then, surprisingly, along with the screams could be heard laughter.

Hearing laughter, Jean slowed to a crawl, not knowing what on earth was going on.

The laughter was clearer now, voices speaking Spanish, water splashing. Jean inched his way closer. Using the cypress trees as cover, Jean moved closer still.

Leaving the levee, he walked through the trees.

Normally, knee-deep water surrounded the span of cypress trees, now, however, the ground was dry due to unusually low amounts of rainfall. Jean was able to proceed with relative ease, but extreme caution.

Ahead, Jean could detect movement in the distance

as the screams grew stronger. Then finally, Jean moved to within 25 yards of the screams.

Seeing an opening in the trees, Jean could see a small clearing, in the middle of which an area had been enclosed by tin.

Looking in horror, Jean watched as he saw a man suspended over the barricaded area by his bound hands. His pants were torn and bloody; his left leg had been amputated just below the knee cap.

Jean's heart pounded hard in his chest as fear weighed heavy in his stomach. Three men surrounded the suspended man, all laughing and speaking Spanish.

One of the three men, a short stocky man wearing jeans and a sleeveless tee shirt, operated the winch that was mounted to a tree. This allowed the operator to raise or lower its load into the pit. The other two men wore blue jeans, and short-sleeved shirts. One wore a pullover, the other a button up, which he kept half–unbuttoned, exposing several gold chains around his neck. All were armed with machine guns.

The man operating the winch once again began to lower the screaming man into the pit, all the while the man pleaded with his captors to shoot him and get it over with. His captors just laughed, they obviously got too much enjoyment out of the torture to prematurely terminate it with a bullet.

As the man was lowered into the pit, the splashing he had heard earlier resumed.

Straining to see the source of the man's torment, Jean stood totally erect, using a large cypress tree as cover.

Jean looked in horror at the inhumanity of the man's torture, as he realized what was in the pit. ALLIGATORS!

The pit had two five-foot alligators, each competing with the other for a larger share of the man's dangling limbs.

The pit's water had been transformed from brown to a light crimson, which had splashed onto the surrounding tin barricades.

The alligators waited for their prey to be lowered closer, while the man defiantly shook his mangled and severed limbs in desperation, spattering blood on his capturers' faces and clothing.

Unfazed, the tormentors lowered the man till his mangled limbs were just above the water. The alligators lunged forward, their razor sharp teeth tore large hunks of flesh as they latched their powerful jaws and twisted their bodies until whatever their jaws had closed around had broken free.

It didn't take Jean long to understand why the man had not bleed to death sooner; Jean noticed that a tourniquet had been tied to each of the man's legs to prevent him from bleeding to death too quickly, thus prolonging the torture.

The hoist operator was given the order to hoist the man up, by the man with the open shirt and expensive jewelry. He shouted at his captive in Spanish then paused as though he were asking him a question and waiting for an answer.

However, from Jean's point of view, the man was not going to be able to answer any more questions ever again.

The man now hung motionless. Using a stick, the man with the gold chains lifted his head to see his face better. Either he decided the man was dead, or in such a state that he would no longer be able to answer questions or provide any more entertainment.

The rope was cut, and the alligators were finally served the full course, as his lifeless body fell into the pit.

Jean was horrified; he had never witnessed such inhumanity, even animals were put out of their misery as quickly as possible. Jean's hands trembled uncontrollably as he perspired with fear. He had to get out of there, now!

Hastily turning to leave, Jean tripped over a large fallen branch, which he had not seen earlier.

He sprawled across the ground, making a loud racket as the branch broke, carrying its noise to the sadistic trio.

Alerted to the noise, one of the trio responded with a barrage of machine gunfire. Lead projectiles tore and splintered as they ricocheted off the surrounding trees.

After falling, Jean knew he was found out, he quickly crawled over to a small fallen tree, lying flat as the barrage of gunfire continued.

When the firing stopped, Jean took the opportunity to make a run for it. As long as he kept enough distance between himself and his pursuers, the thick cypress should provide cover from any clear shots.

First, he had to misdirect them. If he broke for the levee and tried to make a run for the boat, he would be gunned down in seconds. His only chance was to get them to chase him, then circle back to the airboat.

Jean was a good bit older than the trio were, but he had kept himself in good physical condition. Plus his knowledge of the swamp and his keen sense of direction would play a vital role.

Seeing Jean jump up and run, the trio shot again.

Jean had moved quickly to get as many trees between him and the gunman as he possibly could. The trees acted as a natural barrier, denying his assailants a clear shot.

Running through the woods, Jean could have easily lost them, but that was not what he wanted to do. If they were to lose him, they might possibly search the levee and spot his airboat, thus eliminating his only means of escape.

"Help!" Jean screamed, knowing there would be none. He only yelled to assist his pursuers in tracking him. Jean yelled and ran until he felt the men tracking him were deep enough in the woods. Jean then quickly and quietly started back for his airboat.

Reaching the airboat, Jean had no time to lose. Jerking the rope that prevented the boat from drifting, Jean sent the paddle along with some shells flying into the air with the paddle conveniently landing inside the boat. Jean spun the front end of the boat around then climbed in.

Machine gunfire could be heard in the distance, as bullets whizzed by Jean's head. Looking down the levee, Jean spotted one of the three men running, still several hundred yards away. He had apparently anticipated Jean circling back and positioned himself on the levee to cover it. Staying as low as possible, Jean reached up and turned the ignition, the engine came to life. Using his right hand, Jean pressed the foot pedal surging the craft forward. With his other hand, Jean operated the shaft used for steering, peering out over the bow to determine direction. After quickly covering a hundred yards or so, Jean jumped into the chair and headed for help.

Hearing the gunfire and the sound of the airboat engine, the remaining two men trailing Jean ran to the levee just in time to see Jean speed away.

"Quickly!" the gold-clad sadist yelled, "Call ahead and have him stopped!"

Keeping the accelerator pedal pushed to the fullest extent possible, Jean took the turns at top speed, the centrifugal force nearly pushing him up on the opposite bank.

"I have to get to a phone!" Jean thought, "Call the Sheriff and have his men pick up these animals!"

As Jean sped through the narrow bayou his thoughts were on the tortured man he had just seen killed. What were they tying to find out, he wondered.

Jean approached the dog-leg bend in the bayou that passed right in front of the main entrance to the plant.

What Jean saw as he rounded the bend made him let off the accelerator and turn the craft hard to the right sending it sliding sideways several yards before coming to a stop.

Chapter Eight

Up ahead in front of the main entrance to the plant, two of the speedboats that had been such a nuisance to him in the past now blocked the bayou. The operators of the speedboats now stood on the bow with machine-guns in hand. Jean considered turning around and heading in the opposite direction when he noticed two men, apparently from the tower, setting up position on the point. The muzzles of their machine guns were pointing in his direction.

"Put your hands up!" one of the men from the speedboat shouted.

Jean must have paused momentarily, because before he could respond to the first command, a second one followed.

"Now!" the gunman said, in a much more agitated tone.

By now, Jean's airboat had drifted to the bank as he complied with his capturers' orders, raising his hands above his head.

The camouflaged duo that had previously held their position at the point now rushed over to the airboat. Reaching the boat, they climbed in and threw Jean to the deck.

With Jean on the deck, both of the men began

kicking him several times, Jean's hands were then bound. With the help of both guards, Jean was lifted into one of the speedboats, which had just pulled up alongside. One of the two men stayed aboard Jean's boat, the other went aboard the speedboat and held the barrel of his gun to Jean's head.

Heading to the steel gate that provided the only entrance to the plant, the speedboat operator pressed a remote control switch and the gates parted, half folding inward with a slow smooth motion.

Once through the gate, the speedboat throttled up its powerful engine, sending the craft sliding through the water far faster than Jean had ever traveled on water before. The blown engine produced such a loud noise, it brought pain to Jean's ears. Not having the advantage of ear plugs like the other occupants, he sat and bore his discomfort in silence.

Looking back at the gate, Jean could see his airboat being brought through the gate along with the remaining speedboat. Once through, the gate slowly closed, once more barricading the canal from unwanted entry.

The speedboat soon arrived at the old Slickco plant, offering Jean his first good look. The facility had been transformed from an oil producing facility to an armed military compound. A twelve-foot, electric, chain link fence surrounded the entire five-acre compound. Located at the main gate, a lookout tower with powerful searchlights was mounted on the railings. Three rows of razor wire was deployed in front of the electric fence; two rows on the bottom and one row on the top of the other two, forming a pyramid-shaped deterrent. Finally, another coil of razor wire was stretched along the top of the fence, completely encircling the camp. Inside the compound, the incoming oil and gas lines were the only recognizable feature of the whole plant. It must have also been of special importance to the owners, for another fence around the receiving lines had been mounted, padlocked, and a guard had been designated to deny access to unauthorized personnel.

The producing vessels along with the portable trailers had all been removed. Replacing the removed equipment stood a large single story building, its stucco structure and red tile roof gave an appearance of Spanish influence. The one oddity that separated this structure from any other structure was the fact that this building had no windows. None. The only visual opening was the large double steel doors located in front of the building.

After tossing a line to the waiting guard, Jean was helped onto the narrow dock. With a guard on each arm, he was brought up to the electric fence.

Waving to the guard in the tower, one of the two guards escorting Jean was given the OK to enter the compound.

They proceeded up to the large steel doors. Each of the guards that held Jean grabbed a door, opening both of the doors together.

Entering the building, you were immediately taken back by the beauty and the luxury of a building, which from the outside gave every appearance of being a warehouse.

Persian rugs were randomly placed across the high polished oak floors. Expensive-looking paintings hung from the finely coordinated wallpaper. Crystal chandeliers hung from the ten-foot ceilings, and the rooms were filled with expensive furniture. The building had been divided into an office / study, bedroom, kitchen, and dining room, the larger of the four rooms being the office. Entering the office, Jean could see a man behind the large oak desk, with his back to them. Seated in a high back chair, only the top of his head could be seen, along with rising swirls of smoke apparently from a cigar.

"Señor Roberto, we got him," said one of the guards.

Swinging around to face the men, Señor Roberto extinguished his cigar in an ashtray on the desk.

Roberto was a native Colombian; having been raised in the poorest parts of town, he knew what it was like to be poor. As a young man, he vowed to elevate himself from his desperate situation by whatever means necessary, and he had accomplished his goal very well. Wealthy and very powerful, he had become the master of his own destiny.

Rising from his leather chair, Roberto walked to the front of the desk, leaning against it, folding his arms across his chest.

His white suit contrasted his brown skin, making him seem much darker than he really was. Señor Roberto had thick black hair, which he wore slicked back. He had small, really piercing brown eyes. His eyes were cold and hard, as though he could pierce your very soul with a stare.

"So, you're the old man causing me so much trouble," said Roberto staring right into his eyes. "What were you doing snooping around this area?" he demanded, his voice much less subdued.

"I was just walking in the woods taking in nature when your men started shooting at me." Jean said, as though looking for an apology.

"What is your name, Gringo?" asked Roberto as he tried to press further.

"Jean Boudreaux," Jean replied.

"Well, Gringo, you picked the wrong area to go exploring nature in," said Roberto, not even a little convinced by Jean's story.

"Did you see anything unusual when you were exploring in the woods?" Roberto demanded, already knowing the answer.

"No nothing!" Jean replied, trying to sound as convincing as possible.

Señor Roberto could tell Jean was lying. He was sweating profusely though the room was very cold, and he appeared to be very nervous.

"Who else knows you're here, Gringo?" Señor Roberto asked, once again not expecting to hear the truth.

"The sheriff, he knows, I told him right where I was going," replied Jean with a little more conviction than before.

"Is that a fact, Señor Jean? You wouldn't lie to me, now would you, amigo?" said Roberto, in a somewhat sarcastic tone.

"Of course I wouldn't," Jean said, realizing what the consequences would be if he wasn't believed.

Just then, the large steel doors could be heard opening once more. Heavy boots tapped their way into the office. Jean turned to see who else was going to enter the room. As he turned, to his surprise the sheriff walked into the room.

"Brad!" Jean yelled in excitement, "Am I glad to see you," Jean exclaimed, breathing a sigh of relief.

The sheriff ignored Jean and walked straight up to

Roberto.

"What the hell did you bring him here for?" said Brad, obviously agitated with Señor Roberto.

"He was trespassing and saw more than he should have," countered Roberto, looking at Jean once again.

Jean realized at that point the Sheriff was working for Señor Roberto. The last hope he had just vanished as they spoke. Jean knew he was a dead man, there would be no way they could let him live, not after what he saw.

"What do you plan to do?" the sheriff asked, more aggravated with the circumstances than concerned about Jean's ultimate fate.

"What we do with all our problems," said Señor Roberto, pausing for a moment then looking straight into Jean's eyes, "Eliminate them."

Fear shot through Jean's entire body. As Jean was being led out the office door, his legs went weak, requiring more assistance from his escorts. The sheriff looked away from Jean as he disappeared through the doors, and back at Roberto.

"You cant be serious, you cant just kill him," the sheriff said.

"I can and I will, He saw us interrogating Chuck at the pit, we can't let him go," explained Roberto, looking at the sheriff with his cold hardened look.

"I won't stand for it," said the sheriff, in a forceful yet

unconfident tone.

"Stand for it?" repeated Señor Roberto. "You won't only stand for it, you will be the one to kill him!" said Señor Roberto, waiting for Brad's response, receiving none, he continued. "You will do exactly as you are told to do. It's about time you started earning all that money I paid you." Reminding Brad of their arrangement.

"And if I want out?" asked Brad.

Roberto laughed as he walked around to the back of his desk and sat down.

"You don't get it, do you? There is no way out for you. I own you. I bought that office that you're in, and I have been paying you quite well, for the little bit you had to do for it. But you remember this, and remember it well. If you ever think about getting any bright ideas about going to the Feds, not only will you die, but your entire family will die. Do I make myself clear!" Roberto concluded, knowing Brad had gotten the message.

"Perfectly," the sheriff replied. "What do you want me to do with him?" he questioned. "He's a well-known man around here. He can't just disappear, too many people will miss him."

"Wait until nightfall, take a couple of my men with you. Bring him and his airboat to the other side of the swamp and make it look like an accident," Roberto instructed.

Brad nodded, sickened by what he had to do. Brad did not like it, but he knew what would happen if he refused. Roberto would kill him, without a doubt.

SOUTHERN JUSTICE

Chapter Nine

The sun felt good on Shad's face as he drove down the Interstate. The wind was blowing his hair from neatly combed to a scattered fluff.

Looking at his fuel gauge, "1/4 tank," he would have to stop soon, he thought.

Shad had been driving three hours without a break or a pit stop. He was getting tired and in need of a quick pickup of hot coffee to help wake him up.

Off the side of the interstate, he noticed a faded billboard in the mist of the tall pines. The sign read:

ETHEL'S TRUCKERS HAVEN

FOOD, DRINKS, AND FUEL NEXT EXIT.

Shad turned off the interstate and headed toward Ethel's.

Ethel's turned out to be a large neon-clad building, with many signs advertising various brands of beer. The corner of the building was cut off at a forty-five degree angle, which accommodated a large glass door. On top of the building, a three-foot high sign read in large letters:

ETHEL'S

Surrounded by a sea of packed gravel, three rows of gasoline pumps were positioned in the front and to the side of the all-metal structure. To the rear, a parking area for eighteen-wheelers.

Shad pulled up to the pump and started filling his vehicle. He noticed Ethel's was relatively quiet for a truck stop just off the main interstate. One big rig in the parking area and three motorcycles parked by the door were the only vehicles in the lot.

Finishing filling his car, Shad secured the nozzle and cap then headed for the building. As he passed the motorcycles, he gave them a thorough examination. They were Harley Davidsons, solid black with stretched handlebars and high polished chrome throughout. Shad could see the immaculate condition the bikes were being kept in. Keeping that much chrome that polished required a lot of work.

Opening the glass door then crossing the threshold of the dimly-lit interior, Shad was immediately confronted from the side with the sinister sound of a pistol being cocked back and something hard being pressed to his head.

"Freeze, or I'll blow your head off," growled a voice just out of his sight.

His eyes had not quiet adjusted to the dim surrounding so Shad thought it best he take the advice of his assailant so he did not move.

"Up against the wall," said the voice, this time adding a shove to the request.

Shad was pushed in the corner with four other

people. A heavy-set, middle-aged woman wearing an apron, probably Ethel, he thought, a gray-haired man wearing all white with a chef hat, and a pretty young blond girl with shoulder-length hair wearing a flowered dress and a large name tag that said "Sue".

They were all trying to be of some comfort to a large man who lay unconscious on the floor. The man showed little signs of life. Blood oozed from a gash in his forehead, his mouth, and nose. He had apparently been beaten almost to death.

"What's going on?" Shad asked as he began to scan the surrounding area.

Sue spoke first, "They came in here about twenty minutes ago, started getting loud and making vulgar advances toward me. That's when Ethel asked them to leave." Sue began to relay the story through broken sobs and tears. Shad had to pay close attention to understand what she was saying.

"Instead of leaving, one of them grabbed me by the waist. Burt here," looking down at the beaten man, "came to my aid." She was crying more now, possibly overcome with a sense of guilt.

Sue gathered her composure, then continued. "They pulled pistols and began to beat him and beat him. Even when he was down, the tall one sat on his chest and swung furiously at him until his fist could no longer deliver the blows. They are crazy!" Sue cried.

Shad's eyes had focused now. He could see the room and the three men clearly now. One sat at the bar drinking a beer, his pistol lying on the counter beside him. Medium built with a slight potbelly, he was the quietest of the three.

The other two bandits were at a table not far from the bar; one standing, the other sitting. Lighting a cigarette, the one sitting seemed only to be laughing and agreeing with his tall companion, who shared his attention between being a lookout at the door and a source of amusement for his comrade.

Yelling, shouting obscenities, and waving his pistol, the tall bandit seemed to be on some drug-induced high, which made him far less predictable, and the situation all the more desperate. All three wore blue Jean jackets with the sleeves cut off, shoulder length hair, and scraggly beards.

Kicking a table, and sending it flying into another, the tall bandit began looking at Sue and grabbing his crotch.

"Come on, baby, let's party," said the biker as he began to slowly move toward her.

"Oh God!" Sue cried, as she cowered behind Shad, understanding what he had in mind.

Shad stood straight, his arms loosely folded across

his chest, as the human parasite walked toward him.

"What you think you gonna do, boy, protect her?" the biker asked as he walked up to Shad.

Seeing the other two still watching and laughing, Shad braced himself as their partner approached. Lifting his gun, he placed it directly under Shad's chin.

"I'm gonna blow your head off!" he shouted.

Shad looked into his face, his eyes were bloodshot, he perspired profusely and reeked of body odor.

"Beg for your life!" the gunman told Shad, applying a little more force to the gun, raising Shad's chin slightly.

Shad said nothing as he glanced around the room to reconfirm the position of the other two men. Then with lightning speed, Shad unfolded his arms and slapped his tormentor's arm to the side discharging the pistol into the wall behind him, barely missing his face but ringing his ears with the loud blast. In the same motion, Shad grabbed his arm, spinning him around and slamming his back to the wall. Now Shad's back was to the gunman's chest and the bandit's arm and gun was in front of him. Throwing an elbow behind him, Shad landed squarely on the bandit's jaw, momentarily dazing him. Not wasting time to remove the gun from his hand, Shad pointed the gun and fired at the other two bandits, using his assailant's own finger to depress the trigger.

They were watching as the altercation occurred, but

it happened so fast that neither one of them had time to react. The last thing they saw as they reached for their pistols was a muzzle flash and a fire-like pain. The impact of the bullets threw them backward, landing haphazardly as everything slowed down then went black.

After shooting his opponents two companions, Shad once again threw a elbow behind him, striking his opponent on the jaw, dazing him still further.

His vice-like grip on the pistol did not allow Shad to remove it. Repositioning the biker's arm from under his armpit to above his shoulder, and with one sudden jerk, Shad heard and felt the biker's arm crack, thus allowing the pistol to fall harmlessly from his hand, on to the floor.

Turning, Shad faced the man, who not more than a few seconds earlier had held his life in jeopardy. The man's face was red, though not bleeding from the two blows, he cried in agony over his broken arm.

Shad straightened him up by his blue jean jacket, "This just ain't your day." Then with a solid right cross landing hard on his chin, Shad sent him flying across a table unconscious.

"Ya'll all right?" Shad asked, turning to the three terrorized people.

"Yes," Sue said softly, as she sobbed uncontrollably, leaning on Ethel's shoulder.

"Look out!" the old cook shouted, "Behind you."

Spinning around, Shad saw the tall punk standing not far behind him. His right arm hung uselessly by his side while his left hand brandished a knife.

"I'm going to cut your heart out," the biker said, as he slowly began moving toward Shad.

Shad did not move. His hands by his side, Shad waited for his attacker to make the first move. They stood and stared at each other for only a few seconds, though it seemed much longer. With a rapid swish, the biker lunged at Shad, swinging the knife in a left to right motion. Shad stepped back, but had misjudged his distance to the wall as his back made contact, not allowing any further retreat. The blade sliced though Shad's shirt and cut into his chest, though not deep, just enough to draw blood.

As the knife passed by, Shad grabbed the biker's arm with both hands. Now Shad held his wrist in the air, ducking under his opponent's wrist, he positioned himself to the side of his assailant and with a quick downward thrust, buried the knife into the biker's chest. The biker fell backward, dead.

Shad walked over to the bar to call the police, stepping over the two lifeless bodies along the way. They had been killed quickly. One had been shot through the head, the other in the chest. Pools of blood had began to form around the bodies as they lay waiting for their final disposer.

Going over to the side of the bar, Shad reached over and picked up the receiver, dialing zero.

A woman's voice came through the receiver, "Operator, may I help you."

"Yes ma'm," Shad responded, "I need the police and a couple of ambulance over at Ethel's truck stop, there's been a shooting."

Not waiting for a response, Shad just laid the receiver on the counter.

Walking back to the rest of the party, Shad was met halfway there by Sue, a first aid kit in her hand.

"Sit down," she told Shad, much more in control than she had previously been. She began bandaging his bloody chest.

The police arrived soon after, with their sirens blasting and lights flashing. They cautiously entered the building with their guns pulled, quickly scanning the area. Finally, one of the officers walked up to Ethel, who began to explain what happened.

It took a total of about two hours before Shad was finally able to leave. Between checking him out with the base and taking his statement, it progressed at a snail's pace. As Shad was leaving, Ethel and the cook, who he had found out was named Elmer, walked up to him and thanked him.

"You promise us you will stop on your way back," they requested, determined not to take no for an answer.

Shad agreed, then turned to Sue, who had not left his side.

"Do you think you can recommend a hotel for the night?" Shad asked.

"I've got just the place," she said, walking Shad out to his car.

SOUTHERN JUSTICE

Chapter Ten

Shad drove through the small community, as Sue directed him with rights and lefts. They did not have to drive far before they arrived in front of a large two-story Victorian home. Immaculately maintained, everything was in order. Freshly painted, with flowers hanging from pots suspended from the porch. The well-manicured lawn only served to broadcast an overall picture of wealth and privilege.

"You live here!" Shad asked, caught off guard by the house.

"Sure do," Sue said, with a giggle in her voice. "Something didn't fit," Shad thought, why would anyone with such obvious wealth be working at Ethel's.

Postponing any further questions until later, for now Shad decided to go with the flow and see where it took him.

As Shad and Sue walked up the drive, Sue passed the walk leading to the front door. At first, Shad did not think this strange, many people used rear entrances only. It wasn't until they reached the rear of the house before Shad started putting it all together.

Walking past the rear entrance, Sue continued to lead Shad. Sue led him to a stairway located on the side of the garage, which led to an upstairs apartment.

"You had me going for a minute," Shad said, as he walked into her apartment. "I thought you owned this place?"

"Did that make you feel uncomfortable," Sue asked, knowing how some people are intimidated by money.

"To be perfectly honest," Shad said, "I never met a rich person I liked. They're very arrogant, I guess money does that to you. I don't know, I never had any."

Sue just smiled, if there was one thing she didn't want to do, it was make Shad feel uncomfortable around her. She saw no need to volunteer that this estate was actually her mother's house. She lived in the garage apartment to give her a sense of privacy. As far as Shad had to know, she was renting from some wealthy widow woman. He did not have to know that this wealthy widow woman she rented from was Ethel, and Ethel was her mom. Was it necessary for Shad to know she only helped her mom at the truck stop in between semester breaks. Did he need to know she was a Pre-Med student at Mississippi State. Sue pondered all this before deciding to keep it to herself. She did not want Shad to be intimidated by her wealth. So if he thought she was just a waitress working at a greasy spoon, and living on top of a garage, that would be OK for now.

As Shad stepped inside Sue's apartment, he noticed how neat everything was. Freshly vacuumed carpet spread from wall to wall. The furnishing was simple but of very good quality. Only a couple of pictures hung on the wall. One of a middle aged man apparently Sue's father, the other a photograph of Sue and Ethel.

"You've known Ethel a long time?" Shad asked, still oblivious to their relationship.

"All my life," said Sue flipping off the response, being careful not to volunteer anything at this point, but also careful not to be caught in a lie.

"Can I get you a drink?" Sue asked from the kitchen.

"Sure, I'll have a beer if you got one," Shad said, as he sat on the couch.

"Here you go," said Sue, handing Shad a beer.

"Dinner will be ready in a minute." Sue prepared many of her meals in advance, so she was able to set a table in a relatively short period of time.

Sue returned to the kitchen and continued the preparation for the meal. Grilled sirloin, corn on the cob, and a huge baked potato completed the menu.

"How do you like your steak?" Sue called out to Shad from the kitchen.

"Medium," Shad called back. Getting up from the couch, he went into the kitchen where Sue was busily working.

"How's it coming?" he asked, trying to make small talk.

"Just fine," said Sue, staying focused on what she was doing. "Was your dad expecting you home tonight?" she asked, not knowing Shad had left early and was not expected yet.

"No, he wasn't expecting me for a couple more days," Shad offered.

"I overheard one of the officers say you were with some kind of special operations," Sue asked, not knowing if he could even talk about it or not.

"That's right," Shad said, "I'm with the Teams."

"Teams?" Sue repeated, more confused than before. "What's a Team?"

Shad had forgotten that everyday lingo which is use by servicemen is not generally used or known by the general public.

"I'm sorry," Shad apologized for not making himself clear. "I'm with the Navy Seal Teams."

"Sounds like an exciting job," Sue commented, as she set the table.

"Just a lot of training," continued Shad, not wanting to go into any great detail about his job.

The couple sat down to eat, exchanging casual chitchat throughout the course of evening. Then at the end of the meal, Sue brought out a bottle of wine with two glasses and a corkscrew.

"Would you open this?" she asked, sitting down on

the couch next to Shad.

Twisting the corkscrew into the cork, Shad removed the cork from the bottle with one easy pull. Pouring each of them a glass, he handed one to Sue.

Shad had waited for Sue to take the first drink, but instead, she paused to make a toast, lifting her glass to Shad's.

"To my gallant Navy Seal who rescued me from the clutches of those awful bikers." Sue concluded the toast by lightly tapping Shad's glass with hers.

Shad brought the glass to his lips, and slowly sipped the wine. It was extremely dry, Shad thought, but Shad was by no way a connoisseur of wines. On the contrary, he hardly ever touched them, he was more of a beer kind of guy. Not wanting to insult his host, Shad quietly sat and drank his wine.

After a few minutes, the conversation tapered off, as Sue and Shad's eyes met once more, locking together as though they were being held together by some invisible force. Slowly, Shad removed Sue's wine glass from her hand and placed both glasses on the coffee table, never for one second removing his eyes from hers. He leaned over and softly kissed Sue. Slowly at first, then becoming firmer stronger, more passionate as their bodies warmed to each other. He wasted no time, picking Sue up off the couch, he carried her to the bedroom, where the fires of their desire could finally be extinguished.

SOUTHERN JUSTICE

Chapter Eleven

The next day, Shad got an early start. Stopping only for coffee and a Danish at a local convenience store, then he was on his way. The time passed quickly, and soon he was crossing the Louisiana State Line. "Only three more hours to go," Shad thought as his car sped toward its final destination.

Hammond, Holden, Walker, Denham Springs, Baton Rouge, the familiar road signs passed by one by one, until finally he was at the St. Martinville exit, which would take him to St. Martinville.

St. Martinville is located at the edge of the Atchafalaya, and had only one road providing access to the community.

The narrow blacktop road had a ripple effect due to settling. Shad reduced speed to lessen the bounce of the heavy automobile.

Turning into the parking lot of his dad's tour business at 11:15 in the morning, two police cars were parked out front, with one police officer standing by the front door. "What's happened," Shad thought, totally oblivious to what was about to be communicated to him.

As Shad approached the door, the officer showed no sign of expression, his mirrored shades concealed his eyes, making it difficult for Shad to read him. Shad nodded as he started to reach for the doorknob of his father's business.

Just then, the officer, who until that point had remained more like a statue than a living breathing human, stuck his hand out on Shad's chest and pushed him back, hard.

"They're closed!" the officer growled.

Rage built up inside of Shad as he fought to control his anger. Finally, he spoke.

"I would think an officer of the law would have better manners," Shad replied, stepping back.

With one hand on his half drawn Billy club, the cocky officer removed his sunglasses to his pocket.

The officer was a fair size man, weighing approximately one hundred ninety, to one hundred ninety-five pounds. With the same height as Shad, they stood eye to eye.

Seeing the officer start to pull out his baton, Shad took one step back and prepared himself for what seemed to be an imminent attack.

"Boy, you got about five seconds to get off this porch, or I'll show you some southern manners you won't forget any time soon," snarled the officer, still holding his baton half-drawn by his side.

Shad was very taken back by this officer; he did not fear him, for he feared no man. What he couldn't understand was how such an obvious bully could not only get a job as a deputy, but was able to keep his job.

Shad's dad had written and told him how the local police force had changed since Depp Leblanc, the town's thirty-year sheriff had died. The new sheriff had run against him, and had won by default after Depp's death, leaving Brad Young the sheriff's office, to do with as he pleased.

Hearing the racket outside, Sheriff Young opened the door coming out on the porch.

"What's going on out here!" he demanded.

"I told this boy they were closed, but he wants to get smart," the young deputy responded.

"Sheriff," Shad started, "My name is Shad Boudreaux. This is my dad's place, could you tell me what's going on?" Both officers' faces suddenly changed expression as Sheriff Young directed Shad to go inside.

Upon entering the small office, Shad saw Mrs. Galliano crying.

"Shad, oh Shad," she wailed.

"What's wrong?" Shad asked, totally baffled by the strange goings-on.

"Your dad," Mrs. Galliano finally managed to explain the source of her pain.

A cold sweat broke out over Shad as he felt his chest cavity descend to his stomach; he had suddenly realized what this was all about.

"How?" Shad asked, tying to maintain his composure.

"Boating accident," Young cut in. "He was out along the area of Alligator Bayou when he must have slipped, hit his head, fell overboard and drowned. We'll know more when the autopsy comes in," Sheriff Young concluded.

"Boating accident!" Shad exploded, "you got to be kidding me!"

"That's the way it looks," the sheriff reiterated his findings.

"The autopsy should be complete by tomorrow, you can take charge of the body and make the necessary arrangements then."

"I want to see him now!" Shad responded.

"The body has already been identified by Mrs. Galliano, and the autopsy has already started.," the sheriff explained, hoping to discourage Shad.

"I want to see him now!" Shad repeated himself.

"Very well," said the sheriff, giving into Shad's request. "But autopsies aren't a pretty sight, I'll wait for you outside." Then he and the deputy turned and left the small office and waited on the porch.

Turning to Mrs. Galliano, Shad tried to reassure her. "I'll take care of everything from here, Mrs. Galliano, you lock up and go home. I'll call you later."

Mrs. Galliano, still tearful, lifted her head. "I tried to call you," she said, "but you had already left." Mrs. Galliano tried to explain through tear-filled speech.

"That doesn't matter now," said Shad, "I'll be back later." With that, Shad left the office, meeting the sheriff and the deputy on the porch.

"Get in the squad car, I'll drive you over there," the deputy said.

"I'll follow you," Shad countered, not waiting for a reply, he headed for his convertible.

The drive did not take long before they were in front of the two-story brick building that housed the sheriff's office and the morgue.

They went through the massive doors and down the long corridor to the end of the hall, then to the basement. As they walked, their heels echoed off the walls resounding throughout the corridor.

"Well," said Sheriff Young, when they reached the halfway point of the hall. "my Deputy will take you from here."

"Thank you," Shad said graciously, extending his hand toward the sheriff.

After descending two flights of stairs, Shad and the deputy found themselves in front of a frosted glass door. Written on it in bold black letters, it said:

Morgue

Just under it in smaller letters was printed:

Dr. A.C. SAVOY

PATHOLOGIST

The deputy walked in without announcing himself in any way, Shad followed.

The morgue was a large un-partitioned room. On the far wall were rows of pull out drawers used to keep the bodies in the freshest state possible while waiting their turn for autopsy. Just inside the door to the left was a rather cluttered desk with a couple of plants just behind it. On the opposite wall was an elevator obviously used to bring in and to remove the bodies. In the center of the room held a marble examination table on which the autopsies were conducted. Above the table were lights, and to the side was a stainless steel rolling table, which held the tools which were used in the autopsy. Dr. Savoy was found on the phone at his desk, just hanging up as they walked in. Wearing his bloodstained rubber apron, he came around his desk and approached them.

"What brings you down here, Deputy?" he asked as he went to shake hands with him.

"The body brought in this morning," the deputy said in a cold insensitive fashion. "This is his son, he wants to see him."

Savoy was not as surprised as he should have been, Shad thought as he listened to the doctor's response. "It is very irregular to view the body after an autopsy has started!" Savoy said, making a feeble attempt at a protest.

"Sheriff Young has given his ok," the deputy reassured him. "He wants to see him so let him see him."

"Very well, over here," replied the doctor, hardly even acknowledging Shad's presence.

The doctor walked to the marble examination table, then around the opposite side. Pulling back the sheet, Dr. Savoy revealed Shad's father's body.

Shad was not prepared for what he saw. Barely recognizable, his dad lay on the marble slab. The skin from behind his head had been pulled to his forehead allowing removal of the top of the skull to the brain. His chest lay severed from just below the throat to the xiphoid process, and slightly parted. Shad teary-eyed, still asked Dr. Savoy his findings thus far.

"It is still preliminary," Dr. Savoy started, "but it looks to support the sheriff's theory. A blow to the back of the head caused cerebral hemorrhage and death."

Peering over his father's body, something unusual caught his eye. Looking at his father's side, Shad noticed a large bruised area. Palpating the area, he could tell at least one of the ribs were broken. "What did you find in this area here?" Shad questioned, indicating the rib area.

The doctor walked around to Shad's vantage point,

then looked intensively at the ribs.

"Yes," said Dr. Savoy, "he probably cracked the rib when he fell," suggested the doctor in the most convincing tone he could muster.

"Isn't it true, Doctor, that bruising ceases upon death," Shad questioned, already knowing the answer.

"Why-ah--yes," Savoy reluctantly agreed.

"Well if what you said is true, Doctor, that the injury occurred when he fell, how would you explain the size of the bruise?" said Shad, pausing only for a moment then continuing. "It appears to me this bruise happened at least a couple of hours before he died."

"What in the hell makes you qualified to make such a diagnosis?" said Savoy, the anger very evident in his voice.

"Well," Shad started, "I had enough of them in my life, many in the same area we're talking about and I know how long it takes to look like this one," concluded Shad, pointing to the side of his father's body. Savoy, obviously baffled by what Shad had said, could offer no reasonable explanation, nothing to contradict his findings.

Finally, Savoy said the only thing he could say in his position. He retreated back into his training and the office in which he had been entrusted and simply said, "Well, those are MY findings," and said nothing further.

Shad began to sense something was wrong, but

couldn't quite understand what it was.

"How long till you release the body?" Shad inquired, as Dr. Savoy replaced the white sheet covering his dad's body.

"Tomorrow morning should be about right," the doctor responded, walking around from behind the table.

"I'll make arrangements for him to be picked up," Shad said, visually shaken up by the appearance of his dad. Teary-eyed and weak, Shad headed back out the door and up the steps, the deputy remained behind to talk to Dr. Savoy.

Leaving the courthouse, Shad headed straight for Mr. Thibidaux's. As he drove, his mind reflected back to thoughts of his dad. The happy times they shared together when he was a boy, and the grief they both shared when they lost his mother, and the day he left for the navy, how proud his dad was. He felt guilty how so many years were condensed into so few memories.

Mr. Thibidaux's funeral home was not far from the courthouse, and within a short time Shad pulled into the blacktop parking lot.

After parking his car, Shad headed for the double wide wooden doors, which acted as a side entrance to the funeral home. Mr. Thibidaux's funeral home had been around for many years and buried all of the small community's loved ones.

Entering the lobby brought back memories of his mother. He was only 12 when she had died and the pain had never really left him. He remembered the beauty of his mother and how she loved him. Always taking time to teach him about nature and life. Taken slowly by cancer, her loss left an enormous void in Shad's life. His father tried the best he could to fill the void and Shad loved him for it. But his strong reassuring hand was not the same as his mother's gentle embrace. Now, once again this building, which held some of the most painful memories for Shad, would house yet another, that of his father.

Shad's reflections were severed with the appearance of Mr. Thibidaux, the owner of the funeral home. Mr. Thibidaux was an elderly man in his late sixties, and had known Shad all his life.

"Shad," Mr. Thibidaux said, "I'm sorry for your loss. Your dad was a great man."

"Thank you," said Shad, graciously accepting his condolences.

Mr. Thibidaux proved to be immensely helpful in making all the arrangements and even helped select the casket.

"When will I be allowed to claim Jean's body?" Mr. Thibidaux asked in a low subdued voice.

"Tomorrow morning at the morgue," said Shad, remaining in control of his emotions.

"We should plan to have the funeral on Wednesday," Mr. Thibidaux suggested. "That would give enough time for visitation," he explained, and Shad agreed. Thanking Mr. Thibidaux, Shad shook his hand and turned to leave.

Outside, the sun was starting to disappear behind the distant trees, as nightfall quickly fell upon the swamp.

Heading to his dad's house Shad was once again bombarded by the memories. Every small shop and playground he passed brought back memories of he and his father playing, talking together, sharing the afternoons. Reflections and regrets was what now haunted Shad. Regrets for not expressing what many sons have trouble expressing to their fathers. Love. Always thinking there is time, but time, like the morning dew, evaporates before our eyes never to come again.

SOUTHERN JUSTICE

SOUTHERN JUSTICE

Chapter Twelve

When Shad turned into the parking lot of his father's business, the sun had completely set, but the moon and stars had not yet appeared. Located next to the business, his father's house now stood vacant.

The large Acadian style home was nestled among cypress trees both front and sides, with a narrow gravel path leading to the 80-year-old cypress structure.

Upon entering the house, one would not be taken back by lavish furnishing. On the contrary, the home was simply furnished with plain furnishings. On either side of the den fireplace were bookshelves, and on one side against the wall was a free-standing gun case. A rifle, shotgun and a pistol inventoried the entire collection. One wall, however, was devoted to something both Shad and his dad had taken a great deal of pride in. That was the mounted heads which hung on the wall. Several large bucks that had fallen to the skillful hunting of he and his dad. All of the trophy heads were of Whitetail Deer, all of which Shad had seen before. All but one. Hanging on the wall about chest height was a set of large antlers mounted on a board. Shad could not help but notice the unusual shape and size of the tines. Not to mention the sharpness of the tines.

Shad looked around the house as though

familiarizing himself with a place he had never been before. In fact, he had only been there a few times since his dad had moved there, and it had been quite a while since the last time. Jean had moved into the house and started his tour business after Shad went into the service. The empty nest syndrome had forced Shad to set new goals for himself that would give him purpose. Getting older, he had found it increasingly more difficult to walk a trap line or any other activity that would require bending, or a lot and lifting. So when the Cajun craze hit and tourists started coming to La in increased numbers, the tour business tapped not only his knowledge of the swamp, but his love for it as well.

Entering a small bedroom just down the hall, Shad set his bag down at the foot of the bed. This had been the room he had stayed in on his previous visits, but now it had changed somewhat. Several framed photographs now hung on the wall. Some were of Shad in high school, but most of them were of he and his father taken on camp outs and fishing trips. On a small end table, an open scrapbook lay with loose newspaper clippings not yet set into place. The scrapbook contained every write up Shad had ever had printed on him, from high school to his various decorations he received while in the service. The room screamed a father's pride in his son, and it hit Shad so hard he broke down and cried as though this was his first opportunity he had to grieve for his father.

Awaking early the next morning by a light continuous rapping on glass, Shad rolled out of bed. Grabbing a pair of short pants and pulling them on, Bare foot, bare chest and somewhat groggy from lack of sleep, he stumbled to the source of the relentless tapping. Pulling the door open so hard it slammed against the opposite wall, Shad was ready to verbally assault the early morning intruder. When he realized who it was, all the anger and steam drained from his body.

Standing at the door holding a box of donuts was Mrs. Galliano, her pleasant disarming smile made Shad feel awful about how close he had come to insulting her.

"Good morning," Mrs. Galliano said, followed by her cheery smile, "I brought donuts."

"Would you like to come in?" asked Shad, inviting her into the living room. "Excuse me while I put on a shirt?" Not waiting for her to respond, he left for the bedroom.

"I'm going to make some coffee," Shad announced on returning to the living room.

"How do you like yours?" he questioned, walking to the kitchen.

"Black!" she replied, setting the donut box on the coffee table as she surveyed the room. Mrs. Galliano had not worked for Jean for very long, only about eight months. She had responded to an ad in the paper for a bookkeeper and all-around assistant. Having had some bookkeeping experience and not quite sure of the latter, she applied for the job.

Jean and Mrs. Galliano had hit it off from the start. It wasn't long before Jean wondered how he had ever gotten along without her. The job was more than just a god's send for Jean. Mrs. Galliano was given new purpose for her life. Since retirement from the school system, then the sudden death of her husband, there had been an enormous void and lack of a sense of purpose in her life. Having only one son, and him being grown and moved away, she was soon overwhelmed by an empty, lonely, meaningless existence. Going to work for Jean rejuvenated her spirit and she was once again a happy and fulfilled woman.

Shad returned with two cups of coffee and handed one to Mrs. Galliano.

"Dreadful about your father's accident," Mrs. Galliano said. "He was a good man and you couldn't ask for a better boss," she continued. "He was very excited about your coming home, he talked about it every day," she replied.

"Yes," Shad replied, "strange how things work out."

"Well, I just came by to see if there was anything I could do. I understand he will be on display tonight?"

questioned Mrs. Galliano.

"That's correct," Shad said.

"Is there anyone staying up with you tonight?" she questioned.

"No, there's no one else," Shad responded, almost forgetting about the tradition of keeping someone up with the dead all night.

"Then I'll stay up with you," offered Mrs. Galliano.

"Thank you, Mrs. Galliano but ..."

"No buts," Mrs. Galliano cut in, "it's settled, I'll see you tonight."

Rising from her chair, Mrs. Galliano headed straight for the door, trying to make a quick exit before Shad could think of an excuse not to let her stay up.

Staying up with the dead was an old tradition dating back for as long as anyone could remember. No one ever seemed to know why they would do it. It was like so many traditions around these parts, you just did it, you did not question it.

Shad spent the rest of the day looking through his father's things, and trying to cope with his grief. The day passed rather quickly, and before Shad knew it, it was time to go to the funeral home. Shad dressed then left for the funeral home about 6 o'clock. He was supposed to meet with Mr. Thibidaux to iron out the final arrangements, and Mrs. Galliano to spend the long night together. The first part of the night passed rather quickly, as many of the local townspeople came by to pay their last respects to a man many of them had known all their lives. The last half of the night would prove more difficult, as Shad fought off the fatigue and exhaustion as long as he could until finally falling asleep on the couch next to Mrs. Galliano.

When morning arrived, Shad and Mrs. Galliano headed home to clean up. The funeral was only a few hours away.

The funeral seemed as though it was being viewed through another person's eyes. Visions mostly blurry and hazy around the edges. Going through the motions, but not yet fully accepting the death of his father. Shad's father's death seemed to bring the realization of his own mortality into focus.

Standing by the open grave after the services had concluded, the townspeople filed by offering their condolences. Shad never realized how well liked his dad really was. This gathering was by far the largest the small town had ever seen.

Even with the obvious distraction, Shad, ever observant of his surroundings noticed two official-looking gentlemen standing a good distance from the proceeding. Dark suits and sunglasses, they stood motionless with their hands folded across their chest as though waiting for someone or something. As queer as he thought the observation was, Shad tried not to be distracted by it.

Finally, the last mourner approached, an old man wearing a suit that was probably as old as he was. Shad recognized him as Claude Breaux an old friend of his dad's. He appeared visibly shaken as he approached Shad with his outstretched hand.

"Shad," Claude started, "I am truly saddened by your loss, your dad and me were friends for as long as I can remember."

"I know, Claude," said Shad, trying to put the old trapper at ease. "You've been a good friend to us both."

"I've got to tell you, Shad, this so-called accident weren't no accident!" Claude said in a subdued tone.

Shocked by what he said, Shad pressed further "Why do you say that, Claude?" asked Shad, determined to get to the bottom of his story.

"I spoke to your dad the evening before he died. He called me asking me a lot of questions about the old plant in the basin."

"You mean the old Slickco Plant?" asked Shad, trying to stay as clear on the facts as possible.

"Yea, that's the one, it has been bought up recently, no one knows for sure who's the big money behind it though. Your dad asked a lot of questions about the speedboats." Claude paused just long enough for Shad to repeat his last words.

"Speedboats?" Shad repeated, not understanding the connection, and obviously puzzled.

"Yea, they run up and down the bayous real fast, and the men riding in them don't appear to be boy scouts, and the guns they, ...well, it ain't no shotgun."

"What does the sheriff say about that?" asked Shad.

"Several of the local townspeople that live along the bayou, including your father, reported it, but the sheriff only said he would look into it. Nothing was ever done."

"Does anyone know where these boats come from?" asked Shad, still not sure how speedboats fit into his father's death.

"Yea, they're kept at the old plant," Claude offered.

"Did my father ask you anything else?" Shad questioned, not wanting to leave any stones unturned.

"No, but he gave me the impression he was heading out there for a look even after I tried to talk him out of it. You see, Shad, a lot has changed around here since you left. We got a new sheriff elected about six months ago. He came out of nowhere, and was up and elected sheriff. First thing he did after getting elected was to replace the deputies with his own people, out of towners that no one knew. They're bad ones, Shad, nothing more than bullies with badges, you watch them. I've had some run ins with them when I went too close to that plant. They really scared me, they did. I thought they were really going to hurt me, I feel I got off easy, they just threw my traps into the bayou and warned me not to show up around there again, or else. I understood clearly what the or else meant, and have stayed clear ever since."

"Is there anything else you can tell me?" Shad pressed further.

"No, that's about it, but you be careful, there are a lot of strangers coming in and out lately, they can't be up to no good," said Claude, in a somewhat paranoid tone.

With that, Claude shook Shad's hand once more and he was off.

Shad looked down once more at the coffin as the attendants lowered it into the earth. Turning away, he started walking to his car. From the corner of his eye, he saw the dark-suited duo closing in on him. Reaching his car, Shad heard one of the men call after him, "Lieutenant Boudreaux!"

SOUTHERN JUSTICE

Chapter Thirteen

"Lt. Boudreaux," the man called, "May we have a word with you?" they asked. Shad did not respond immediately, but turned to face the two men who acted as though they knew him. Still fresh in his mind what Claude had told him, Shad was suspicious of these men's motive, and was not going to let them get too close before finding out more about them.

"That's far enough!" Shad said, in a strong firm voice, taking a defensive posture.

The two strangers stopped dead in their tracks as Shad wheeled around.

"Take it easy, we just want to talk to you." By this time, they had removed their identification.

"I'm John Taylor," the taller of the two said, handing Shad his identification to inspect. "And this is Tim Arnold."

"DEA," Shad said, as he looked the two men over, then handed John back his badge.

"How do you know me?" Shad asked; not yet willing to let his guard down.

"We pulled your file, Lieutenant.," responded the other agent, who until this point had not spoken.

"What business does the DEA have at my father's funeral?" Shad question.

"We are sorry for your loss," replied John, "but we think your father's death may not have been an accident."

"Why do you think that?" Shad asked in a demanding tone.

"What we are about to tell you is strictly confidential," John started. "We have been conducting an investigation into the Slickco plant. There is a strong possibility it may be a drug distribution center."

"Why are you telling me, just go in and bust up the operation," said Shad, offering his simplistic approach to the situation.

"It's not that easy," John continued, "thinking, and having the proof to justify a warrant is quite another story," explained John.

Tim looked around uneasily as though knowing they were being watched, but not knowing from where.

"As of two days ago, we had a man on the inside gathering information," John continued.

"What happened?" Shad asked as he began to feel uneasy about the whole situation.

"His mutilated body was found in the river twenty miles from here. It looked like alligators got him. We think your dad may have accidentally stumbled across something that may have cost him his life," said John, hoping to tie in his father's death with the operation to ensure Shad's cooperation.

"What do you need from me?" Shad asked, as he too began looking around.

"We need you to look around, ask a few questions about the movement and activity of the plant," John replied.

"Why don't you do it?" Shad asked inquisitively.

"We would, but we don't know the swamp for one thing, and for another, every time we try to talk to someone, they clam up tight. Totally uncooperative," summarized John.

"Uncooperative? You expect the people down here to spill their guts to a couple of city strangers? For all they know, you could be the bad guys trying to find out how much they know," said Shad, his argument well made.

"That's exactly our point," said John, "we need you."

"I'll look around and if there's something to find I'll find it. How can I get back in touch with you?" Shad asked, walking around to the other side of his car.

"We're staying at the hotel under the names Smith and Jones," John reported.

"How original," Shad smiled as he got into his car and drove off.

As Shad was leaving the cemetery, he spotted a gray sedan parked with two men sitting inside. They were either waiting for someone or watching someone, Shad thought. His paranoia peaked after his meeting with the DEA agents. As Shad drove by, the two men remained facing forward, not even a glance as Shad passed by. This only made Shad more suspicious, so for the next several blocks, Shad's eyes stayed glued to the rear-view mirror, waiting to catch a glimpse of the car following him but it never came.

Thoughts ran through Shad's mind like a kaleidoscope, one thought overlapping another, blending into one another until he had a collection of thoughts rotating around in his mind.

Heading back to his dad's house, Shad kept looking in his rear-view mirror for a tail. The meeting with the two DEA agents had made him extremely paranoid and yet more focused to find out what was going on around him.

Reaching his dad's house, Shad turned into the shell driveway and parked in front of the house.

Turning off the engine, he could hear in the distance a faint roar of a high-powered speedboat.

He leaped from behind the wheel of the car and ran to the bayou.

Each step he took increased the intensity of the sound, as the speedboat's powerful engines gradually went from a high pitch hum, to a powerful roar. Shad reached the bayou just in time to see a bright red speedboat tear past him, offering only a quick glimpse of it.

Though he only got a brief look at the boat, it had been long enough for him to see only two men occupied the boat, one was the driver and another literally riding shotgun, armed with what appeared to be a high-powered rifle. Hardly out for a pleasure cruise. Shad reasoned that nothing he could immediately gain access to could keep up with the jet. Even if he had a powerful enough boat to pace the jet, it would prove inadequate for surveillance. It would be heard coming from too long a distance, thus alerting the crew that they were being stalked.

Shad knew just what he needed, but it wasn't a boat.

SOUTHERN JUSTICE

Chapter Fourteen

After changing out of his dress clothes into jeans and a pullover shirt, Shad jumped into his car and pointed it out of town.

On the outskirts of town was a small single hangar airfield he once worked at when he was in school. The owner, Shad's former employer and friend, Dirk Derrick was a former green beret who had done two tours of duty in Nam. He was by far the most heavily decorated solider Shad had known on a personal basis.

Pulling up outside the hangar, Shad went inside looking for Dirk and found him waist deep in the engine of a Cessna.

"Need a hand?" Shad asked, as he walked up behind him.

Startled, Dirk jumped up, bumping his head on the shroud.

Dirk Derrick was a slender lanky individual with a good natured personality. Balding on top, Dirk tried to compensate for the thinning top by letting his hair on the sides grow well below his ears. To look at this forty-nine-year-old man, you would guess him to be much older. The scars of Vietnam had taken a heavy toll on him, and it was apparent just by looking at him.

Dirk had bought the airfield shortly after his return

from Vietnam. With only two Cessnas and a glider, it was not much of an airport. Dirk made ends meet by giving flying lessons to bored housewives, most of which came from Lafayette.

"Well I'll be darned!" said Dirk as his facial expressions changed from one of surprise to one of delight.

"How in the heck are you doing?" he asked, as Shad extended his hand to shake, only to have it slapped away. Dirk grabbed Shad, giving him a big bear hug.

"Man, it's great to see you again," said Dirk releasing Shad, thus allowing him to breath once more.

"I'm sorry to hear about your dad, I couldn't go to the funeral because, well you.. ," Dirk tried to offer an explanation.

"You don't have to explain," Shad replied, "I understand."

Since Vietnam, Dirk had not been to a single funeral. Having seen all the dead bodies he cared to see in Nam, Shad reasoned.

"I need a favor," Shad explained, "I need to borrow your glider for an hour or so."

"I'll need to be piggyback over the Atchafalaya and released at about 3,000 ft.," Shad explained.

"Too early for duck season," Dirk questioned, "What are you looking for?"

Having borrowed the glider before to spot pockets of ducks for his dad, Shad would spot the ducks that would find out of the way ponds of water, which were inaccessible by boat. With the use of the glider, Shad was able to guide his dad to the spot.

"You might not want to get involved in this one, Dirk, I'm not even sure what I'm dealing with yet. It could get pretty hairy," Shad cautioned, trying to warn him off.

"I've always been pretty good at minding my own business," Dirk said, "but if you need me, you know where I'll be."

Dirk went to untie the single engine Cessna, which was right outside the hangar.

While Dirk untied the Cessna and started the pre-flight check, Shad went to check out the glider.

Shad had learned to fly the glider from Dirk when he had worked after school around the hangar. Capable of carrying two people and staying aloft for long periods of time, the craft utilized rising wind current, and an extra long wing span, which would selfishly grab the wind to remain aloft.

Opening the small cockpit of the glider, Shad manipulated the joystick to check the flaps. The glider's instrumentation was simple, it had an altimeter, compass, a leveling device, and a radio for two-way communication to the tow plane. After completing the inspection, Shad went to look in the hangar for a towline.

By this time, Dirk had gotten the Cessna started and was heading to the glider. Returning to the plane with a long coil of rope, Shad secured one end to the glider and the other end to the tail of the Cessna, being careful not to tangle the line.

Remembering he did not have his binoculars, he quickly ran back to his car to retrieve them.

Returning to the glider, Shad climbed in the cockpit and strapped himself in, then switching on the radio, he directed Dirk down the runway.

The Cessna roared down the runway towing the glider behind it on the towline.

A slight jerk at first when the last of the towline had been played out, but most of the shock had been absorbed by the long nylon towline.

At full throttle, Shad radioed Dirk to gun the engine to the maximum rpm's, which sent the Cessna speeding down the runway. Shad achieved liftoff first, but maintained a low altitude to prevent putting the tow plane in a twisted position after liftoff.

Shad had forgotten how peaceful flying the glider really was. The only sound was that of the distant Cessna, and the wind passing over the wings of the glider as they ascended to a predetermined altitude.

Soon, they approached the Atchafalaya River and

Shad radioed for the release. Pulling the small handle which secured the towline, Shad released himself from the plane and began to free-fly.

Free-flying now, Shad viewed the landscape below. The brown bayous snaked their way to the gulf, contrasted by the green foliage of the swamp. Even at this height, boats on the brown background of the water stood out in sharp contrast. With the use of the binoculars, the images came in crystal clear.

Lowering to an altitude of about 2,000 ft, Shad followed the twisting bayou that led right in front of his dad's house. It had not been very long since the speedboat roared past him, thirty minutes at the most, he had been hoping to maybe spot him on the return trip, thus narrowing the area in which the boat had traveled.

Several miles ahead, Shad could see an old boat landing which had been shut down and abandoned because of disrepair. Its out of the way location had received little use.

There was a great deal of activity around the landing now though. It appeared there was a car and boat with four people moving about, hauling something.

Shad reached for his binoculars and focused in on the scene below.

Shad was stunned as he peered out his window; right

below him the red speedboat now lay tied to the broken-down dock. Its two occupants were busy transferring small bundles from the back of the boat to an awaiting car. The sheriff's car!

Two deputies helped with the unloading and loading, forming a line passing the bundles from one to the other, finally ending up in the trunk of the sheriff's car.

Shad could not believe his eyes. But now it started to make sense to him. Whatever was going on with the speedboats, the sheriff was in on it.

Keeping his distance, Shad watched the transfer conclude. The sheriff then handed the driver of the boat what appeared to be two small briefcases then got in his car and sped off down the dusty dirt road leading back to town.

The speedboat was also quick to depart, with the white trail of foam and the high roster tail tailing behind. Shad decided to follow the speedboat to see if it made any other stops along the way. The boat sped through the bayou making good time. Traveling much faster than Shad, he was able to keep up with him, but only because of the advantage of not being restricted to the curving bayou. Shad could fly a straight line or even take short cuts across areas he knew the bayou would curve right back to.

Thirty minutes passed when the speedboat slowed.

Shad was not surprised to find himself right above the old Slickco Plant. From the air, however, it did not resemble the old plant at all. The only thing that remained unchanged in the plant was a few rusty vessels. A new building in the center of the plant had been recently constructed and the entire compound had been surrounded by a fence. Three bayous leading to the plant were now blocked in some way. One had been damned up, the other had been filled in with what appeared to be scrap iron, the third had a small guard tower and a fence at the entrance.

The gate slowly opened, as the speedboat approached, turning into the slip leading to the plant.

Shad had seen enough, far more than he had expected. How far did the influence of the plant extend, he wondered. How many people were involved? These thoughts weighed heavy on Shad as he headed back for the airfield.

Making a large circle around the field, Shad leveled out his approach and descended to the strip, making a smooth landing on the asphalt runway.

Seeing Shad land, Dirk hopped into his old pickup and sped to the end of the runway where Shad had stopped, one wing tipping over to the ground balancing the lightweight craft.

By the time Dirk reached Shad, he was already out of

the plane. Dirk pulled up, backing the rear of the truck to the nose of the plane, positioning himself to tow her back.

"How was the flight?" Dirk asked as he got out of his truck and walked back to the glider.

"Very interesting," Shad replied "Dirk, what can you tell me about the local sheriff and his deputies in town now?" Shad questioned.

"Not a whole lot," Dirk started, "the sheriff had just moved here around election time and qualified to run, when Sheriff Leblanc had his accident."

"Accident?" Shad questioned.

"Yea, he was out hunting and must have fallen from his deer stand and shot himself, freak accident. Brad was the only other one running so he won by default." Dirk paused as though in deep thought, looking at the ground and stroking his beard, then he spoke once more.

"Not long after he was elected he replaced all the deputies with his own men. They also were outsiders," said Dirk as though just realizing what he had said.

"Wasn't there any opposition to him replacing the deputies?" Shad asked.

"Sure," said Dirk, "Lots, but there was not a whole lot anyone could do, he was the new sheriff and he had the right to appoint who he wanted."

"One more thing, Dirk, did this happen before or after

the plant was bought?" Shad asked.

"Come to think of it, after," Dirk explained, puzzled and unsure of where Shad was going with this. "What are you getting at, Shad?"

"Don't really know right now? It may be nothing," Shad answered, tying to curve his friend's peaked curiosity.

After getting back to the hangar, Shad helped Dirk position the glider in its space, thanked Dirk for all his help, then he was off again.

SOUTHERN JUSTICE

SOUTHERN JUSTICE

Chapter Fifteen

Thoughts raced through Shad's mind as he headed back into town. What was the connection between the plant and the sheriff's office? What were they transferring from the boat into the trunk of the sheriff's car? And why did the old plant take on the appearance of a fortress? Many pieces to the puzzle, but none seemed to fit together.

Since Shad noticed the sedan at his father's funeral, he had become very observant to his surroundings. This had paid off. As he drove back to town, he noticed a gray four-door sedan with two men in it lagging behind in the distance. Not close enough to arouse the suspicion of anyone not looking for them, but close enough to keep their quarry in sight.

Shad wanted to eliminate any possibility that his paranoia was working overtime. Entering the outskirts of town, he took a right at the first street he came to and maintained a constant speed. Soon, the gray sedan also turned down the same street, maintaining the safe distance from Shad's vehicle that it had before. One more turn, Shad thought, and if he follows, his suspicions would be confirmed. Shad approached the upcoming intersection; barely slowing down Shad negotiated the turn easily, though rather noisily, as his tires screeched on the hot pavement.

The gray sedan sped up now, aware that Shad had made their tail. The sedan tires smoked as the rubber slid around the corner trying to close the gap on Shad. But to their surprise, there was no sign of Shad! He had completely disappeared!

As Shad was turning the corner, he saw the sedan speed up and knew what to do. After rounding the corner, Shad floored the accelerator. The powerful engine responded, pushing Shad against the seat as the car surged forward. About two blocks away, Shad slammed on his brakes, quickly rounding the corner. This would be repeated several more times until Shad's trail was that of a maze, leaving the gray sedan without any idea what direction Shad took, considering there were so many possibilities.

Driving into town, Shad headed for the hotel where the two DEA agents were staying. Two blocks from the hotel, Shad noticed a deputy's patrol car parked to the side with two deputies sitting inside. Just sitting, and looking. Striking Shad as a strange place to take a coffee break, he turned into a side street before passing their car.

After parking, Shad hurriedly made his way back to the corner to observe the deputies further. What Shad had seen from the glider made him very suspicious of the local law enforcement, and he was not going to take any unnecessary chances.

Peering around the corner, Shad could clearly see the two deputies in the patrol car. The driver was the cocky little deputy that Shad had the run in with earlier.

Observing the dash of the patrol car, it was littered with sandwich papers and a couple of coffee cups. It was obvious to Shad that the deputies were on a stakeout that had been in progress a while, and Shad knew right away who was being watched!

Surely, the two DEA agents must have known they were being followed, or did they?

Shad wondered when the surveillance had started?

Was the car he spotted at his father's funeral part of the same surveillance? How careless could these two clowns have been, Shad wondered. Then Shad began wondering how long the tail had been on him? Sure, he had looked, but an individual experienced in following someone is usually not seen, especially when the one being tailed has other things on his mind.

Looking thoroughly now for anything that looked out of the ordinary, Shad walked back to his car and passed it, stepping into an alley which paralleled the street the deputies now watched.

Quickly making his way through the alley, Shad soon came to the service entrance of the hotel. Cutting through the kitchen, Shad was hardly noticed with all the activity going on around him. Stopping to peer through the glass window of the swinging door that led to the dining room, Shad looked for anything out of the ordinary, anyone who seemed out of place, anyone more preoccupied in observing what was going on around them rather than tending to his own business.

Not noticing anyone suspicious, Shad started through the door at the same time a waiter loaded with a tray full of dishes was attempting to go through. A loud thud followed by the crash of dishes breaking on the floor was heard as Shad knocked the waiter down with the door.

So much for being inconspicuous, Shad thought as he helped the fallen waiter to his feet.

The crash had summoned everyone out of the kitchen to see what the commotion was all about.

Deciding enough help was available for cleanup, he quickly slipped away, and out of the dining room, heading for the front desk.

"Could you tell me what room Mr. Smith and Mr. Jones are in?" Shad asked the attendant.

The attendant did not say a word but went right to flipping the pages in the oversized register.

"Room 202," said the attendant, then went back to her card file.

Room 202 was at the top of the stairs, the first room to the right. Knocking softly at first then with a great deal of enthusiasm, Shad pounded on the door. Behind the oak door John's voice could be heard demanding identification.

"Who is it!" John shouted.

"It's Shad, now open this door!" he said, quickly getting agitated by the delay.

The brass key could be heard as it poked its way through the slot and turned the tumbler as the bolt shifted, allowing the door to open.

"Come on in, Shad," John offered as Shad walked right by him.

"Did you guys know you were being watched?" Shad demanded, addressing both John and Tim, who was also in the room.

"A tail!" John reported, unbelieving.

"Yes, a patrol car a block down. I don't know how long they have been tailing you," Shad reported.

"It doesn't much matter at this point," John replied, "we can't do much good out there anyway. How about you, Shad, you find anything out?"

"I think I did," Shad said, "I went for a flight after I spotted a speedboat a friend of my dad's told me about. When I located the boat, it was offloading packages into the sheriff's car."

"It would appear our suspicious was correct about the sheriff's office after all," John said to them, then looked at Shad to continue, when he didn't, John initiated the conversation.

"What's the next step?" John asked, as he studied Shad's face.

"What we do right now is tell me what the heck is going on in this town," Shad demanded, his voice forceful.

"We don't know any more than you do," said John at an attempt at being evasive.

"Well, I'll ask one more time and if I don't hear what I want to hear, I'm heading back to Fort Benning," said Shad, turning toward the door trying to emanate his seriousness.

"Wait Shad!" said John, trying to reason with him. "Much of the information we have is of a secretive and sensitive nature," John said, hoping that would be enough to appease him.

"Fine," Shad said, heading for the door, "you keep your secrets."

"Wait!" begged John, "sit down, we'll talk."

Shad turned away from the door and took a seat in one of the high back chairs positioned directly across from the bed.

"Shad," John started, "what we are about to tell you

is classified information and you must promise to keep it that way."

"You got it," Shad said, as John started his story.

"About six months ago, the Slickco Plant was bought by a company named Estavar Oil. Estavar Oil is a dummy company of a Colombian drug lord by the name of Señor Roberto Hernandez. We suspected he might be using it as a base of operations. We believe we were right; within the last six months, drug activity around here has skyrocketed. Dealers from all over the country have been seen around here. We believed we had a jump on his operations, when we were able to place an undercover operative in the plant. Up until a couple of days ago. I told you about him being found in the river. Unfortunately, he died before he could give us any information. We don't know how he is getting the drugs into the country.

"Since the plant was bought, the Coast Guard has increased patrols on the coast and a fleet of radar blimps were dispatched to detect any low flying planes, but we still have not been able to determine how he is getting his shipments." John concluded his explanation, never once taking his eye off of Shad as though trying to see how effective his story had been.

"I'll have to get a closer look at the plant," Shad replied, "maybe watch it for a couple of days. But first, it's time for you to call in a favor if you are owed one," Shad said, addressing the statement to John, who appeared to be delighted that Shad had agreed to take on the assignment.

"The army has a rather specialized boat which has been adapted to the special needs of the swamps. I'll need you to pull some strings and get that boat here by tonight."

"Tonight!" John exclaimed, "How about a little advance warning," he asked.

"I need it by tonight," Shad repeated himself. "I'll also need an M-16 with extra clips, three Laws rockets, and night-vision.

"My God!" John replied, "We just want you to do surveillance, not blow the place up."

"That's all I intend to do," explained Shad, "But if I get in a situation where I need one, it might just be a little too late to requisition one," Shad said sarcastically.

"The boat will have a military radio on board, you will have to monitor channel thirteen for a report," Shad concluded, in the same casual manner he had maintained throughout the conversation, like it was nothing unusual, nothing out of the ordinary.

"How long before you think you might have something?" John asked.

"Don't know," Shad answered, having stood up and

walked to the door.

"But when I do, you guys had better be ready to move in," Shad said, opening the door and leaving the room.

SOUTHERN JUSTICE

SOUTHERN JUSTICE

Chapter Sixteen

John wasted no time in coordinating the assault team within a quick jumping off point. Lafayette would be the closest he could get without arousing suspicions; it had the agents and equipment he needed. He realized his whole career would be on the line if he fouled this up. Having been one of the DEA's golden boys, John had risen quickly in the organization.

Starting out working undercover, John had been credited with some of the largest drug busts in DEA's history. The total commitment John had to the job came with a heavy price. His wife divorced him, then took their son, then five, back to Boston where she was from. John was devastated by the loss, but he could hardly blame her. She rarely ever saw him when he was working undercover and when she did, the toll the job had taken on him had transformed him into a different person.

Lately, however, John was on a roll, a few recent high dollar drug busts had once again put the shine of the spotlight back on him. This case would be the first case where he was actually the one in charge. Not just an agent taking the risk and doing the job. He was now in a position of responsibility and accountability. John knew if this operation went sour, there would be a hunt for a scapegoat, and he would be at the top of the list.

John had gambled everything on Shad. With his inside man having been killed and the death of Shad's dad, it had appeared Shad had been a godsend. After learning about Shad's dad, John ran a background check on Jean, not knowing at the time if Jean was even involved in the drug operation or not. Through a trace of next of kin, John found out Shad was in the service. But not just any service; an elite Navy Seal division. Contacting Shad's C.O., John was able to ascertain just how specialized Shad really was. Shad's C.O. had reluctantly given John the information he wanted, only after John went above his head, pulling a few strings.

The C.O. had told John that Shad had been on several missions involving reconnaissance, mostly working alone. Shad was able to disappear into the jungle as though becoming part of it. He would then radio out four to five days later for a pickup and have detailed information of his objectives.

"Without a doubt, sir, he is the best recon soldier special operations has," reported Shad's C.O. when questioned about Shad's skills.

That was just what John needed was reconnaissance. To find out how, when and where the drugs were coming in. He knew he did not have enough evidence for a search warrant and without it, anything gained in a raid would just be thrown out. John was putting the whole case on the shoulders of one man. This chilling thought crossed John's mind as he realized the stakes they were playing for. Also, there were intangible agendas that may also be at work, Shad's agenda for instance. Could Shad keep the investigation in a professional context, or was he doing it only to extract justice for his father's death. John pondered the downside of Shad being a loose cannon; it would not only jeopardize the investigation and probably get him killed, it would also most assuredly end John's career. But John realized he had no choice, they were nowhere without Shad.

When Shad entered the alley, it reeked with the stench of trash stacked in bins whose only cleaning had been an occasional heavy rain. Shad wondered why he didn't notice it earlier, maybe he was too preoccupied. Shad soon arrived at his car and brought the engine to life as he accelerated out of his slot and headed back to his dad's to await the boat. It was now mid-afternoon and Shad estimated the boat to arrive around midnight, so he was going to get a few hours sleep before it arrived. For after it arrived, Shad would be off, not knowing when he would sleep again.

Awakened by the telephone around 10:15pm, Shad fumbled for the receiver.

"Hello," Shad said, in a groggy incoherent tone.

"Sir," the voice came through the receiver. "This is

Sergeant Simms, assigned to deliver the boat you requested. We have landed at the Lafayette airport and the boat is being offloaded as we speak, we expect to be at you location at 23:30 hours," concluded the Sergeant.

"Thank you, Sergeant, I'll be waiting," with that, Shad hung up the receiver and got out of bed. After putting a stronger than usual pot of coffee on, Shad took a quick shower then dressed in his black camouflage fatigues.

In the den, Shad went through his father's map drawer looking for the area of the plant. Shad found the large geographical map with what he had hoped for. Bright red marks throughout the map.

Shad's dad had without a doubt the best maps. Where ordinary maps just showed the topographical features, Jean through the years had written notes and arrows of particular hazards that lay in the bayous. Cypress stumps cut just below the water line, which could tear a hole in the bottom of any boat. Fallen trees that had turned an otherwise accessible bayou into a dead end. His dad had also noted large mud banks, which from the surface appeared navigable until you ran high and dry on the bank, helplessly stuck. Shad read each tiny note that had been written by his dad.

In the area surrounding the plant, many notes were refreshing to his memories of years past, some were new and he made a mental note of these. Drinking his last sip of coffee, Shad heard a large truck pull up outside the house. Looking at his watch, he was surprised to realize an hour had passed so quickly. A loud rap on the door redirected Shad's attention as he went to answer it.

Opening the door, Shad found himself face to face with a young sergeant dressed in green fatigues, a clipboard in his hand.

"I'm looking for Lt. Shad Boudreaux," the young sergeant stated, still looking at the clipboard.

"I'm Lt. Boudreaux," he affirmed.

The young sergeant sprung to attention, saluting Shad with a loud 'sir'.

"At ease, soldier," Shad reported.

Shad eyed the soldier as though he was conducting an inspection, all his brass was nice and polished along with his shinny jump boots. The sergeant's neatly pressed uniform revealed a nametag that read Collins.

"Sergeant Collins," Shad started, as the young sergeant relaxed from attention.

"Is everything in order on board?" Shad questioned as he looked out into the parking lot at the 20-foot boat as it was being launched into the slip by two other soldiers.

"Yes sir!" Collins replied, "The vessel is completely fueled and ready to go. In the side compartment, three Laws rockets have been placed, here is your code to gain entry." Collins handed Shad a small piece of paper on which four numbers had been written: 1957. Shad smiled, easy enough to remember he thought, it was the year of his birth.

"Under the front deck," Collins continued, "you'll find your night vision."

"And finally, in a holster beside the seat is the M-16, extra clips will be found in the glove box." Collins concluded, as a loud splash was heard, a result of the boat slipping off the trailer into the water.

"Will there be anything else, sir?" Collins asked as he looked over the paperwork one more time, making sure there wasn't a mistake. The pause was only momentary as Collins continued.

"Ok sir, if you would sign right here indicating you received the boat," Collins said, handing Shad the pen and using his finger to indicate where he was to sign.

Saluting once again, Collins turned and headed back to the awaiting truck, which had already pulled up with the other two men waiting inside.

Closing the door as the truck drove off, Shad returned to the table to pick up the maps and within moments, he was out the door, locking it behind him.

SOUTHERN JUSTICE

Chapter Seventeen

The night was dark and clear; all the stars could be seen in the sky that was void of a moon. A gentle breeze attempted to cool the warm humid night but to no avail. Shad began to lightly perspire as he walked to the boat.

Army green and sleek, in its all aluminum design, the long bow seemed to comprise the whole boat. The small windshield was set back about half the length of the boat. Powered by a high-performance engine, the craft was capable of reaching speeds well over one hundred mph.

But that's not what made the boat special. The boat was specially fitted with two flat plates that resembled skis, and were designed to perform in much the same manner, skimming across the surface of the water. At high speed, the plates were hydraulically deployed away from the bottom of the boat, skimming across the surface, lifting the boat up and decreasing the draft of the boat. The boat had been tested in as little as one foot of water. It was equipped with a flexible shaft which allowed it to be lowered when the boat was elevated, the prop also had the capability of being totally retracted into an inverted "V" shaped slot in the stern upon impact, eliminating damage to the prop. This was accomplished by a heavy-duty plate, approximately two inches wide, which ran from the keel, parallel to the shaft and stopped just below the prop. This retractable feature allowed the boat to jump small levees and sand bars without damaging the prop.

The boat was finally equipped with a muffler system that reduced the exhaust sounds by 75%. This facilitated to a certain degree, silent running.

In the cockpit were sophisticated electronic and digital read outs on water depth, speed, and direction, with a built-in tracking device in case the boat was ever stolen.

Shad climbed on board, placing the maps on the small dashboard. Shad then sat down in the leather wraparound chair.

Before him was a solid dash, no wheel, no instrumentation, so it would appear. To anyone else, the boat would give the appearance of a major screw-up. Designing a million dollar boat and not even putting in a steering wheel.

Lifting a small panel just to his right next to the chair, Shad was able to reveal a keypad. He punched in four numbers, 1-9-5-7. After pressing the last number, the dash split in half, the top half rotating upward then downward with the lower half doing the exact opposite. After the dash had been rotated back, an inner dash rotated 90 degrees then outward about a foot revealing a steering wheel and the electronic panel.

Pressing a small black button on the upper right side of the panel, he started the powerful engine.

After allowing a few minutes for the engine to warm up, he cast the bow and stern lines off, the boat remained close to the dock without the normal current to drift it. Reaching under the console, Shad brought out a small case and set it on his lap. Opening the lid, it revealed what appeared to be a set of goggles with tubes protruding from the eyepiece.

Removing the glasses from the case, Shad pulled them over his head, adjusting the straps to secure them in place. A flip of a switch and the entire landscape went green. Shad was now able to clearly distinguish everything around him.

Replacing the case back under the console, Shad put the boat in gear and slowly started moving away from the dock. He estimated it to be about a thirty-minute boat ride to the plant entrance, as he gunned the engine to full throttle and looked at his watch.

The boat handled nicely as it sliced through the calm brown water of the bayou. The sound of the engine could only be detected as a slight hum with the displacement of the water making more noise than the engine. At night, the swamp came alive; many of the nocturnal animals were on the move. The elusive white tail deer could be seen on the bank under a large oak. Raccoons near the shore enjoyed a midnight meal of crawfish. Movement everywhere, viewed at night with the aid of night vision.

Soon, the observation tower at the main entrance came into view. Shad could clearly see the two guards in the tower, one leaned with his chair against the low wall, head down, asleep. The other guard looked out over the swamp with an uninterested look.

As Shad got closer, the guard's expression changed, he stood up from the edge of the wall and was straining to get a better look at the dark silhouette speeding toward him.

But by the time he realized what was going on, Shad had already passed him, speeding toward the second canal, which had been damned up.

Arriving at the second canal, Shad chose a place just past the canal that his dad had marked on the map. Shad initially passed the small slip, but by doubling back, was able to find it the second time. The slip had apparently been dug for a barge bringing heavy equipment to dig the canal. Over time, brush and small trees had grown up around it concealing the slip from the rest of the bayou. Shad nosed the aluminum craft into the tiny opening. Branches could be heard slapping against the side of the hull as it pressed its way farther in, until finally the craft was completely inside the slip and completely hidden from the bayou. Shutting the engine off, Shad grabbed the M-16 and jumped off the bow onto the soft shoreline. Securing the bowline to a small tree, he headed to the levee where he planned to walk the tree line to the plant.

As Shad approached the shell bank of the levee, he noticed something that seemed out of place against the lighter shell background. Still wearing his night vision, Shad went right to the peculiar sighting. A pair of binoculars lay on the shells, it did not take Shad long to identify the binoculars...THEY WERE HIS DAD'S! Shad had given them to him for Father's Day and had his initials inscribed on them. Shad turned the binoculars over and there was his father's initials: J.L.B.

Keeping low, Shad moved quickly and quietly along the levee, he also began tuning in to his surroundings. Every sound, every movement was quickly being analyzed by Shad.

After a while, Shad arrived at the chain link fence that surrounded the plant. He had a good view from where he was. The large white building, which was positioned toward the center of the plant, was in clear view, along with several guards. The facility had changed quite a bit from what he had remembered. There were still a few wells and vessels located in the plant, but most of the equipment had been removed. A new feature to the plant was a rather large receiver of some sort. A receiver, as Shad had once been told, was used to receive a polypropylene or rubber object, either shaped like a bullet or a ball known in the oilfield as a "pig." This object is launched from one end of an oil line to the other using pressure. As the pig travels down the line, it cleans any paraffin that may have been left behind by the oil. But why, Shad wondered, would they need such a large receiver, and where did the line go to?

Suddenly, without warning, a siren went off and the once small flare on the flare ignited, illuminating the entire area. There was a tremendous amount of activity, three guards ran over to the receiver and waited as though not knowing what to do next. In a minute or two, a door opened to the large white building, revealing a man who walked out, dressed in a white suit and a panama hat. Following him was another older gentleman wearing a lab coat. Both men headed for the receiver.

Upon reaching the receiver, the man in the white suit observed as two of the guards loosened the bolts that held the cover of the receiver in place. As the cover was moved away, the other guard reached into the receiver and pulled out a cylinder about eighteen inches in diameter and about four feet long. Placing the cylinder on the ground, the man dressed in the lab coat knelt over the cylinder and appeared to be removing something from inside. Having completed his task, both the gentleman in the lab coat and the man in the white suit returned to the white building.

Shad moved along the fence trying to get a better look at the cylinder when suddenly the distinctive click of a revolver's hammer being drawn back could be heard just behind Shad's ear.

"You move one inch, Gringo, and I'm going to blow your head off," came the angry voice laced with a heavy Spanish accent.

SOUTHERN JUSTICE

Chapter Eighteen

"Now get up!" the man ordered. Shad slowly rose trying to judge how close the man was to him. He felt sure if the man was alone and within striking distance, he would not have a problem disarming him. As Shad planned his attack, a second man came into view from the corner of his eye. So much for that plan, Shad thought as he placed his hands on top of his head. Shad's two captors kept a safe distance away, preventing Shad from making a move on one or the other. Reaching a gate that had already been opened, Shad was led to the large white building. After entering the building, Shad was brought directly to a large office where the man in the white suit waited for him. Seated behind his desk, the man in the white suit looked up as they entered. Two other guards were in the room, both of which had their rifle sights trained on Shad.

"So," started the man in the white suit, "you are our midnight caller, so to speak. My name is Roberto Hernandez, started Roberto,

"And will you give me the courtesy of your name?" Roberto asked, staring into Shad's expressionless face. Roberto formulated yet another question as a puzzled look crossed his face.

"You look very familiar," Roberto started, "But I just

can't place it. Have we ever met?" he asked.

"No!" Shad replied.

"Well, tell me now," Roberto continued, "what were you doing sneaking around our gate?" he questioned.

Shad did not reply.

"What the hell is THIS?" Roberto asked, holding the night vision hood.

"This is U.S. Government issue," Roberto continued, "You DEA?" he asked, stepping closer to Shad.

With a solid backhand, Roberto struck Shad across the face forcing him to take a step back.

"Gringo, you will find your tongue soon," he said, as he walked back around his desk.

"Take the men and search the area outside the fence, make sure he was alone, and find his boat," Roberto ordered the guard standing next to him.

"Take him and lock him up, we'll see how he holds his tongue tomorrow at the pit," Roberto concluded motioning his men to remove Shad.

"Since you're going to kill me anyway," Shad said, "could I at least die knowing why?" Shad knew what his fate was to be, if he was unsuccessful in an escape. What he wanted now was information; information only Roberto could supply. For if he did manage to escape, he would have a better idea of what he was up against.

Roberto, being an egotistical individual, did not have

to be persuaded. He obviously welcomed any opportunity to brag about what he had accomplished, and how he had outsmarted the DEA.

"Sure, Gringo," said Roberto, caught up in the power he now had over Shad. "What you and your DEA buddies suspect is that this is a drug distribution center. What you don't know is how the drugs are getting in." Roberto spoke with a cocky overtone, as though gloating.

"I know all about the costal surveillance," continued Roberto. "While the DEA was spending all their time looking for boats and planes, I've been steadily shipping in the drugs right under their nose.

"Why do you think I would be so interested in an old oil plant?" Roberto asked, not expecting or even waiting for an answer.

"Pipelines!" Roberto burst out, "Miles and miles of pipelines. All we have to do is get the drugs to one of our offshore platforms. From there, the drugs are packed in specially designed cylinders and sent through the pipeline using high pressure gas."

"That's the purpose of the flare," Shad said, as the remaining pieces to the puzzle were falling into place.

"Now you're catching on," said Roberto. "When we receive a shipment, we have to flare the gas before opening the line.

"After we get the drugs, they are packaged upstairs

then sent out by speedboat," said Roberto, taking a great deal of satisfaction in his organization.

"From the speedboat, it goes to the sheriff," Shad offered, surprising Roberto with the extent of his knowledge.

"That's right, the sheriff has been very helpful in our distribution efforts," said Roberto. "Who is going to search a sheriff's car?" he asked, already knowing the answer. "From there, the Sheriff meets with the dealers to make the transaction, pretty slick, don't you think?

"You DEA, you think you're so smart, you even thought you could plant a spy. But we took care of him the same way we're going to take care of you.

Roberto, smiled as he motioned to the guards to remove Shad.

Shad was led out the office and down a narrow hall until he was facing a steel door. Hands tied and blindfolded, Shad was pushed inside.

From the smell of the various cleaning solutions and the moldy smell of damp mops, Shad realized he was in a dark and damp broom closet. Shad felt around for something he could use to free his bondage.

He groped around for anything that could facilitate his release, but there was nothing, finally, he settled down with the realization that nothing could be done until morning. Hopefully, morning would offer the opportunity for an escape.

Several hours had passed before the steel door opened once more.

"Get up!" the gruff voice ordered, as Shad struggled to get to his feet.

Shad was once again led into the office of Señor Roberto.

"You know," Roberto said, "I've been sitting here thinking where we met before. When in fact, we did not meet." Roberto explained farther. "I placed a call to the sheriff, and he told me Shad Boudreaux fit your description.

"So your Jean's son, come to avenge his father's murder?"

"Murder?" Shad questioned, as though he had blocked out that possibility, even though everything had been pointing to it.

"Yes." Roberto smiled as he began to explain what happen to Shad's dad.

"Your father was nosey like his son. He witnessed two of my men dealing with a DEA spy. So your father had an accident," Roberto concluded.

"You son of a bitch!" Shad yelled, tying to shake free the two guards holding him.

"Now, does anyone else know you're here?" Roberto asked.

"Go to hell!" Shad told Roberto in a defiant voice.

No sooner had the words left his mouth when the bodyguard standing next to Roberto stepped up and drove his fist into Shad's midsection, knocking the wind out of him.

Shad struggled for air, the punch was hard and well placed. The only things that kept him from going down were the two guards, one on each side holding him up by the arms.

"You will talk," Roberto told Shad. "Take him to the pit," Roberto told the two guards, "Find out what he knows." With that, the two guards led Shad out of the office and out of the building.

Once outside, they were joined by a third man, who seemed to be leading the way.

Heading toward the same gate he had come through the night before, in the early morning, however, the compound took on an entirely different look. Shad was able to notice a lot more fortifications than had previously been detected.

Machine gun nest dug into the ground for a low profile to minimize detection. Many more guards were visible now, all attending to their prescribed duties.

As they passed through the gate, Shad wondered about the "pit" which awaited him. He also thought about his dad and how stumbling across the pit cost him his life.

Leaving the levee, they walked single file on narrow boards about ten inches wide, which had been elevated to facilitate dry travel when the swamp had water.

Looking around, Shad noticed the swamp was dry, thick with trees, and had an unusual amount of underbrush.

As the group made their way along the boardwalk, a large opening came into view. In the center of the opening was a corral made of sheets of tin. It was obviously being used to keep something in, but what?

As Shad got closer, he saw the bloody rope suspended above the pit and the distinctive sound of GATOR thrashing about as they detected their approach.

Upon entering the clearing, the leader leaned his rifle against a tree and started untying the rope which hung over the pit.

Nearing the pit now, Shad could see the two large gators thrashing about. The bloodstained ground and tin gave every indication that this site had been used recently.

It appeared Shad would be next.

"How you want to hang him, Carlos?" the man standing closest to Shad asked, talking to the third man, who was struggling trying to untie the rope.

"Hang him like the others," the man instructed,

sounding aggravated.

As it turned out, this would prove to be a big mistake.

Pedro, as Shad had heard him called, was a short man about five feet five inches, with a big belly. He was obviously just a hired gun used to taking orders and not questioning them. Apparently, the other victims of the pit were suspended with their hands over their heads, and because Pedro was going to have to untie Shad's hands from behind his back before he could put them over his head, this would provide the opportunity Shad had been waiting for.

Analyzing the situation, Shad noticed the leader of the trio was still occupied with the rope. The third man had his rifle trained on Shad, and Pedro had laid his rifle on the ground to untie Shad's hands. Seeing an opening, he was about to make his move.

As Pedro untied Shad's hands, he said, "Ok, Gringo, you don't try anything funny or my friend here will blow your balls off. You'll still go in the pit, only without balls," Pedro said, laughing as though what he had said was extremely funny.

"Hurry up!" the third man shouted as though he could not wait for the fun to begin.

Pedro was still laughing as he walked around the front of Shad.

Shad waited until Pedro was directly between him

and the third man. With the speed and the force of a charging linebacker, Shad grabbed Pedro catching him off balance and pushed him into the third man, who was also caught totally off guard. As Pedro fell backward, the rifle must have been jarred, discharging a round into the back of Pedro and exiting inches away from Shad as both men went sprawling to the ground. Shad dashed quickly into the swamp as he heard the sound of bullets whizzing close by, apparently from the leader's rifle. Snaking his way through the trees, he soon had enough trees between himself and the gun. Stopping dead in his tracks, he listened. He could hear the leader shouting at the third man.

"You idiot!" Shad heard him shout. "Get back to the camp and tell them what happened. Tell them to get the boats and block the bayou, everything must be covered. If he gets away," the leader said, still shouting. "We're going to be the next ones to be lowered into the pit. Now go!"

The leader had apparently decided to pursue Shad on his own. Shad knew he could take him out, that wasn't the problem. The problem was time. With the third man going back for reinforcements, Shad's only chance was to make it back to his boat before all the escape routes had been sealed off, and hope they did not find his boat before he did.

Running quickly through the swamp, Shad stopped every so often to determine the leader's distance and direction. Apparently, the leader was not in the best of shape, or he was too cautious in his pursuit. For every time Shad would check the leader's location, he would get farther and farther away.

Breaking out into the open as Shad came to the edge of the bayou, he stopped to catch his breath. Shad could hear the leader in the distance as he fought his way through the swamp.

What was more disturbing to Shad, however, was what he heard in the distance. The faint hum was growing increasingly louder as Shad turned and ran once again to his boat. The hum Shad had heard in the distance was one of the jet boats coming to cut off his retreat. Shad reached his boat just as the jet boat arrived on the scene. The boat's occupants each pointed their automatic rifles toward the levee in anticipation of Shad's appearance.

Moving cautiously and slowly, Shad climbed into the boat, untying the bow rope as he went. The speedboat was less than thirty yards away when the leader burst into the open, almost being shot by the guards in the boat.

Shad knew he had to act quickly. If the leader searched the tree line, he would surely be found. Shad moved to the console and pressed the black button that brought the engine screaming to submission. No sooner had the engine turned over, Shad threw it in reverse and gunned it full throttle, turning the wheel a hard right.

The boat jumped from its hiding place tearing out a couple of small trees in the process. When Shad had turned the boat hard right, he SET IT ON A COLLISION COURSE WITH THE SPEEDBOAT!

SOUTHERN JUSTICE

SOUTHERN JUSTICE

Chapter Nineteen

It worked beautifully, before the speedboat knew what happened, they were hit by Shad's boat knocking them off balance, with one off the gunman going into the water. The leader, on the other hand, had acted a little faster firing his rifle in the direction of Shad's boat.

Shad had remained down and didn't get up as the bullets pierced the aluminum and embedded itself harmlessly into the Kevlar shroud that surrounded the cockpit.

After impact, Shad threw the boat into forward gear and gunned it, causing the boat to leap forward, throwing him against the seat. Raising his head just high enough to peer over the bow of the boat, Shad turned the boat toward the center of the bayou as he sped off. He was speeding down the bayou with a comfortable lead on the speedboat when suddenly, once again shots rang out, this time shattering the small windshield.

Looking up ahead and to his right, and there, halfway into the bend of the bayou was the second speedboat. Shad slowed so he could make a sharp turn. He edged the bow as close as he dared to the bank, temporarily losing sight of the jet boat. Spinning the wheel as hard to the right as it would go, Shad gunned the engine, kicking up soft mud as the bow responded and spun around.

Just then, the jet boat appeared in the bend slinging lead toward Shad. Shad once again went to full throttle. Retracing the path from where he had come, only now, swerving to prevent the jet boat from getting too good a bead on him. As Shad passed the first jet boat, the driver was helping his wet counterpart into the boat, with the man on the bank still yelling.

Turning to the console, Shad found the switch that would activate the deflector shields. The bullets seemed to be getting closer when one finally shattered what was left of the windshield. Shad found the switch and flipped it upward. Looking behind, Shad watched as a solid steel panel rose from the rear decking, coming to a stop at a forty-five-degree angle. The jet boat no longer had a line of fire on him. The elevated plate rose to a height just above his head. The shield was not designed to stop bullets; a much thicker plate would have been required for that. The design was to deflect the bullets harmlessly out of the way, thus the forty-five-degree angles. He could hear the abuse the deflector was getting as he reduced his swerving and straightened his course.

Both boats were pretty evenly matched for speed, and neither one was able to get an advantage on the other. Shad's only chance was to disable his pursuers' boat. Shad mentally went back to his dad's map, trying to recall a natural obstacle that would be of use.

Remembering back to his dad's map, he remembered a note with a line drawn across a narrow bayou. Shad took the left at the fork in the bayou and headed for it. He knew what bayou it was, he also remembered how easy it was to pass up. Keeping a sharp eye out for it until finally the entrance came into view. Shad would have to make a sharp ninety-degree turn into the bayou at a high rate of speed. The chances of Shad slamming the boat into the opposite bank were pretty good, but he was going to have to try. He hugged the left bank as close as he felt he could, the water was shallow and mud churned from behind the boat rather than the usual white foam. Shad was almost even with the entrance when he turned the wheel as far to the right as it would allow. The boat veered in response, with the right side of the boat nearly touching the water, the left side kicking up into the air. Shad had timed the turn just right. When he leveled off, he was straight in the middle of the small bayou. The jet boat had slowed, unwilling to risk such an aggressive maneuver, and it entered the bayou at half-speed giving Shad a small lead.

He was rapidly approaching the fallen log that his map had indicated. Not wanting to hit it at full throttle, Shad pulled back to half throttle. He felt the boat strike the log, sending the bow upward. The force catapulted the boat out of the water, sending it airborne for about twenty-five yards. The boat splashed down hard, jarring Shad as it impacted. Shad once again gunned the throttle, sending the boat racing ahead.

When Shad felt he was a safe enough distance from the log, he slowed then turned just in time to see the jet hit the log. Not having the knowledge of the log as Shad had, the jet hit it at full speed. The tandem tore away from the boat as it was catapulted upward. The fuel tanks ignited, engulfing the entire hull, finally it disintegrated as it landed hard on the muddy bayou water.

During the hot pursuit, Shad had not had time to even think about calling John, but now Shad thought would be a good time.

"Little Goose calling Mother Goose," called Shad, transmitting his predetermined code. Shad waited for a while with no response, then just as he began to repeat his transmission, he heard a response.

"This is Mother Goose!" John's familiar voice came back.

Hearing John's transmission, Shad responded, "The Goose is loose." This was Shad and John's predetermined code to launch the attack.

"Roger," John's voice cracked through the speaker. The assault team was now activated. The only thing Shad had to do was to stay alive until it was all over.

Simple, Shad thought as he slowly made his way through the bayou, deactivating the deflector shields so he could see behind him without standing up. Looking behind him in the direction of the burning boat, he could see black smoke growing thicker and thicker as the flames began to engulf more and more of the fiberglass hull.

The bayou he found himself in was was actually a cut through for the two merging bayous, which met at the fork where he had turned earlier.

Emerging from the cut, he had every intention of waiting for the DEA to wrap up the operation, when in the distance Shad heard the other jet boat. It was still a good ways away; the sound of the powerful engine gave away its location.

"Not again!" Shad thought, as he pushed the throttle forward. It did not take long for Shad to reach top speed, but unlike the other jet boat, this one was closing on him. Shots rang out but passed harmlessly by as Shad redeployed the deflector shields. Shad was not going to be able to outmaneuver this boat as he had the last. With this boat being so much faster, he would make up the time quickly. Shad had now left the area where his father had marked full of hidden hazards. It seemed Shad was all out of tricks as he swerved hard right, preventing the jet from getting alongside him.

Coming into an area he was familiar with now; a marshy area of the basin he had duck hunted in when he was off on leave. Shad remembered an area that was high and dry in low tide, and on high tide the solid bottom was submerged by about two feet of water. Shad realized this to be his only chance, as the jet boat became more and more aggressive.

Going back to the console panel, Shad deployed the skies. Slowly, the boat was elevated above the water with only the prop submerged for thrust. He closed in on the grassy shore, not all together sure this maneuver would work. After all, the boat was still experimental.

Hitting the shore, he progressed uninhibited across the plane. As long as he maintained his speed, he was fine. The jet boat was not as lucky. Hitting the shore at such a high rate of speed, the boat was sent upwards then crashing down on its side, jettisoning its occupants into the shallow grass bank.

About this time, Shad heard helicopters overhead. The DEA's assault would soon begin, Shad thought as he left the grass and reentered another bayou, retracting the skies and slowing the boat to idle.

Shad started back to the plant just in case he could be of some assistance. As he neared, the sound of gunfire could be heard. In the distance, Shad could see the helicopters making their strafing runs. Suddenly, one of the helicopters burst into flames, obviously having been hit by a rocket.

The compound had been much more fortified than even he had expected, and the DEA in an effort to maintain secrecy may have bitten off a bit more than they could chew.

Gunning the boat, forcing it to respond forward, Shad pressed a button, which slid the passenger seat back revealing the Laws rockets. Picking up one of the rockets, Shad pulled the rocket to an expanded open position, and he positioned the rocket on his shoulder as he approached the guard tower. The tower had apparently been the reason for the ill-fated aircraft, as Shad could see one of the guards arming another rocket.

Sighting in on the tower, Shad pressed the trigger. The rocket shot out of its tube and quickly found its target. The tower was now engulfed in a huge fireball, the explosion sent debris flying just as Shad negotiated the turn, crashing through the barricade as debris fell downward.

Two helicopters remained, strafing the area but unable to secure a landing site, their fifty caliber machine guns blasting the landscape as Shad approached the dock.

Grabbing one of the remaining rockets, Shad leaped from the boat. Kneeling on the dock, he took aim on the second tower. Soon, it too was engulfed in flames. This would now allow the helicopters a landing spot unimpeded by the elevated vantage point of the tower.

As Shad made his way up the dock, a dead gunman lay sprawled on the dock, his automatic weapon by his side.

Two guards suddenly appeared from behind a large storage tank and took aim on Shad. Instinctively, he dove to the ground rolling, finally landing just behind the dead guard's body, as bullets sprayed the area. Some buried themselves harmlessly into the deck boards, others pierced the dead guard's body, unable to inflict any more harm. Shad grabbed the guard's rifles and rolled on his side to his back, then to his stomach again, firing as he rolled. The spray of bullets sent a barrage of lead into the unsuspecting guards, who fell to the ground dead.

Picking himself up from the deck, Shad ran to the gate and peered into the courtyard. Chaos abounded; there were guards running here and there, not knowing really what to do. For many, the indecisiveness cost them their lives, as the helicopters now dominated the engagement with machine gunfire. Pushing his way through the gate, Shad ran for the white building through the smoke and the gunfire. The thirty yards Shad had to cover seemed like the longest yards he had ever ran.

Reaching the door, Shad stopped himself by letting his back slam against the wall. He peered into the courtyard, making sure no one had followed him around the building. The gunfire seemed to be lessening as the DEA agents began neutralizing key defensive positions. Shad's back hit the door hard as he threw himself against it, ducking into the wide doorway to avoid any stray bullets.

Shad reached for the doorknob, it was locked.

Stepping back, he shot the lock and door handle, splintering the wood around them. With one quick kick, he opened the door then quickly stepped to one side.

Just in time! No sooner had Shad kicked opened the door, a barrage of bullets came flying straight at him. The bullets missed Shad, but just barely as he pressed his back to the wall once more.

With one hand holding the rifle, Shad eased it around the corner, only exposing the rifle and his hand to any further gunfire. Shad let off several rounds in a sweeping pattern. Then still firing, Shad dove to the floor and looked for the gunman.

There was no one in sight!

Shad lay there for a moment, peering down the hall but no one showed themselves. Rolling to the wall, Shad rose to his feet, slowly moving toward Señor Roberto's office.

Reaching the office door, Shad heard the sound of the bolt of a machine gun being operated back and forth. Shad immediately knew what had happened, the rifle had jammed on him!

Entering the room, Shad began his search to find Roberto wrestling with his Uzi, but to no avail.

Seeing Shad, Señor Roberto dropped his gun and raised his hands. "Don't shoot," he begged as he backed up against the wall. Shad walked closer as he sensed the fear swelling up inside of Señor Roberto.

"You killed my father!" Shad yelled as he held the gun to his face.

"No!" Roberto shouted, "It wasn't me. It was the sheriff, he did it," Roberto pleaded as he trembled with fear.

"But you ordered it," Shad shouted. "Now open your mouth."

"What!" said Roberto.

"I said open your mouth!" Shad said, slamming the rifle butt against the side of Roberto's head, sending him sprawling across the floor, stunned.

Picking him up by the shoulder, Shad once again echoed his demand, except this time Roberto reluctantly complied.

Shad stuck the barrel of the rifle into Roberto's mouth then pulled the bolt back, pushing a bullet into the chamber. Tears ran down Roberto's face, as his cries for mercy were muffled by the rifle in his mouth.

Just then, John burst into the room, "Shad, it's over," John shouted, not daring to come any closer.

"Why should I let this slime live? What's the justice in that!" Shad yelled.

"We need him, Shad," John explained, as he maneuvered himself so he could make eye contact with Shad. "With him, we could bring the whole southern drug distribution to its knees. Imagine, Shad, the first Colombian drug lord caught on American soil," John pleaded, looking for some type of favorable response.

Slowly, reluctantly, Shad removed the barrel from Roberto's mouth. Grabbing him by the shoulder, he pushed him to John, who in turn handed him over to two other DEA agents that had just entered the room.

"What about the sheriff?" Shad asked, throwing the machine gun down on Roberto's desk.

"All his deputies have been rounded up and are safely behind bars," John explained, hoping this would be enough to appease Shad.

"What about the sheriff!" Shad demanded once again.

"We don't have him yet, Shad, but it's just a matter of time. We think he high-tailed it up to Lafayette," John said, as he put his revolver back in its holster as they were walking out the building.

Outside, the aftermath of the battle looked as though someone had dropped a bomb on the location. One of the lookout towers was completely destroyed, another smoking, 55- gallon drums were scattered everywhere. By the fence were the rounded-up Colombian prisoners on their knees, with their hands on their heads. A nearby DEA agent was pointing a gun at them. About a quarter of a mile away was the smoldering remains of the helicopter that was shot down during the battle.

"We've called in for transportation," John said, also looking around. "Man," John continued, "what a mess. This place was a fortress." He looked toward Shad.

"We can't thank you enough," John said, hoping to convey his sincere gratitude for what Shad had accomplished.

Shad said nothing as his thoughts were still on the sheriff.

"Can we give you a ride into town?" John offered.

"No thank you, John," Shad said, "I'll take the boat."

Walking away toward the boat, which he had left at the dock, Shad climbed aboard, once again firing up the engines, bringing them to a roar.

Heading down the bayou, Shad passed the remains of the tower he had blown up a short time earlier. A smothering pile of debris giving no resemblance to a tower was all that remained. Clearing the gate, he gunned the engine toward town.

Feeling good, Shad was happy he had been able to bring down such an evil operation. Then, on the other hand, saddened that such an organization could operate with complete secrecy and immunity. Then an innocent man, a good man stumbled across such unexpected evil and it cost him his life.

SOUTHERN JUSTICE

Chapter Twenty

Shad's knuckles were turning white from gripping the steering wheel so hard at the thought of his father's death.

The boat slid though the waiter effortlessly, and soon Shad had arrived at his father's dock. Securing both bow and stern lines, Shad headed to the cabin to call for the boat to be picked up.

As Shad headed for the house, his eyes caught the sign mounted on top of his dad's office. Swamp Tours. Shad realized how many people would no longer have the opportunity to view the swamps through the eyes of a true Cajun. Someone who could tell you things about the swamp no one else knew. Sure, someone else would fill the void created by his dad's death, but no one could truly take his place. He was a Louisiana original.

Shad reached into his pocket for the key at the same time he reached for the doorknob. All he could think of now was a hot shower and some sleep. But as he grabbed the doorknob, it pushed forward... the door was open!

"Did I leave it open?" he wondered. Entering the room, an uneasy feeling came over him. "Something's not right," he thought, but it was too late, he had let his guard down and now he was caught, trapped. He slowly turned and saw Brad standing less than five feet away, holding his revolver on Shad.

"You had to mess it up, didn't you?" said Brad, in a visibly distraught state. "We had a sweet deal going until your dad had to stick his nose where it didn't belong," continued Brad.

"So you killed him," Shad said, staring hard at the sheriff, his anger rising to a point of total eruption.

"That's right!" the sheriff said callously, "I killed him, Just like I'm going to kill you," he concluded.

Shad's anger was starting to override his better judgment. Shad started considering an all out rush, thinking he would not be able to kill him, even if one of the bullets did hit its intended mark. Instead, Shad decided to bide his time and wait for an opening.

"How does it feel to know you're going to die," the sheriff asked.

"I don't know, why don't you tell me?" Shad said, in a defiant tone.

"You forget, I've got the gun," said Brad, as though Shad was not aware of it. "Aren't you going to pray like your dad did? Proud man though, he wouldn't beg for his life," the sheriff said, stepping across to Shad and pointing the gun at his head.

"Will you beg?" the sheriff continued, staring into Shad's eyes.

Staring into the sheriff's eyes, they were cold and cruel; eyes that would have pierced right through anyone else, but Shad just stared back.

"Beg!" the sheriff yelled, stepping still closer to Shad, "I want to see you beg!"

It could not have worked out better if Shad had planned it himself, the sheriff was now within striking distance, as Shad moved to disarm him.

With lightning speed, Shad came up with a forearm while simultaneously twisting sideways out of the line of fire. The pistol fired, sending its projectile harmlessly into the cabin wall.

The force of the blow Shad delivered sent the pistol flying across the room, coming to rest under a small end table.

Shad followed through with his left fist, catching the sheriff just below the rib cage, bending him over in pain. A right uppercut followed it, sending the sheriff sprawling across the floor.

The sheriff got to his feet quickly and brandished a knife, Shad was not sure where it had come from. He lashed out at Shad, catching him by surprise. The razor sharp blade sliced through his shirt, cutting deep into his arm. He jerked back as the blood oozed from his arm.

It had happened so quickly and Shad's adrenaline was flowing so that he felt no pain as he positioned himself in a defensive karate stance.

The sheriff came at him once more, this time with a downward stabbing motion.

Catching the sheriff's right hand with his left, Shad spun under his opponent's arm, causing it to twist behind his back, making him drop the knife.

Pushing the sheriff toward the wall, he slipped on Shad's blood on the way, sending him reeling, landing hard on the floor.

The sheriff got up once more, much slower this time as Shad approached him.

Lashing out at the sheriff with a barrage of blows, Shad quickly turned the sheriff's face into a bloody mess.

The sheriff made a last ditch effort in a move that would prove fatal for him.

As Shad started to turn away, the sheriff picked up a cane which was in the umbrella rack and started at Shad.

Stopping him before he had gained too much ground on him, Shad made a running jump kick, catching the sheriff squarely on the chest and lifting him off the floor.

The sheriff was catapulted toward the wall of trophy heads, stopping short as the tines of his father's trophy buck pierced his back, tearing through his chest. The sheriff fell to the ground, dead.

"Now! That's what I call Justice! Southern style!"

Shad said, standing back to admire what he had just done.

It was over now; the last piece of the puzzle had been put in place. Shad looked around his dad's place and realized that this was no longer his home. What had made it so for so many years was now gone, and sadly, the place no longer would hold him as before. Shad reflected further to his new home, that of the service, and a blonde-haired girl named Sue in Mississippi. He would soon be sent on another assignment for his country, in some foreign land, but it would be some time before he could ever forget this homecoming.

THE END

SOUTHERN JUSTICE

SOUTHERN JUSTICE

OTHER GREAT TITLES BY

Ricardo S. Dubois

Ghost Squirrel

Swamp Witch

A Time for Miracles

Crossroads

The Treasure of Jean Lafitte

Vengeance is Mine

Southern Justice

Lighter Than Air

Turnabout

The Mardi Gras Murders

Titles available through Amazon Books, or Autograph
copies available by contacting me at:
craftycajun@yahoo.com

www.ingramcontent.com/pod-product-compliance
Lightning Source LLC
Chambersburg PA
CBHW020612250626

47154CB00004B/1472